# Junkyard Lucy

**By Tony Nesca**

**<u>Chapbooks</u>**

**Stale Anchovy Kisses -**

**Dead Bats Amidst The Bullshit Laughter And The Lovestricken Cockroaches –**

**Hollow Man –**

**La Gioconda -**

**Charlie -**

**Mondo Cane -**

**<u>Novels, Short Stories, Poetry</u>**

**Dishpig -**

**About A Girl -**

**Emma Strunk -**

**Jukebox Music -**

**La Gioconda (the novel) -**

**The Do-Nothing Boys -**

**Bulletproof Smile -**

**Vodka Orange Sunday -**

**Hobo –**

**Crazy Legs –**

**Junkyard Lucy -**

**<u>Screamin' Skull Press</u>**

**Screamingskullpress.net**

# Junkyard Lucy

## Tony Nesca

*Don't you know there ain't no devil, it's just god when he's drunk.*

*Tom Waits -*

*Life is the farce which everyone has to perform.*
*Arthur Rimbaud -*

**This is a work of fiction -**

# THE LEDGE

No rain -

He sat up there sweating into the hot summer night not a breeze, not a wisp of air, barely a sound...eighteen stories down among the trashcans and the disfigured sidewalks and the bloody alleyways and the well-trimmed lawns and the money-bag corvettes and the long-lost bus-stops garbage strewn all over the streets side to side with the lost and the fulfilled and the almost-crazy, people running and cruising and missing the target always - maybe this was right, maybe it was time...on the ledge he felt alone and happy and the brick and mortar against his back was cool almost sultry and nothing in this poorly-lit world could take that away from him, nothing, below all quiet and small full of terror and fire and ice, his regrets swam around him and the cloudless sky was black like velvet, crescent moon down low arching over the skyline horizon all orange and distant and beautiful in its decay his hangover working perfectly with all this and his alone-ness like a blanket taking him to that right place... "I'm not afraid" he said looking down then up – "I'm not afraid" he repeated.

Looking back it hadn't been all bad, not at all, it was the boredom mainly, the sheer repetition and routine and continual drive to consume, to participate, to accomplish, to acquire things, always THINGS, new smart phones, new computers, new cars, more suits and ties, another house, video games, pop music, superhero boots, lawnmowers, cigarettes, designer drugs, toys layered over toys over gadgets over electric wanderings no-win solutions and no more G.I. Joe with the Kung-Fu Grip – and the waiting, goddamn, the endless waiting – waiting at bus-stops, waiting at restaurants, waiting in line at the grocers, at coffee shops, at movie theatres, at that infernal doctor's office, waiting for something in your life to change, anything, just sitting and waiting and thinking and…then there was the failed marriage, there was that, but it wasn't his fault, no fucking way he said out loud, and even his children turned out to be boring and predictable and in the end far too uninteresting – the tears filling his eyes he said, "My name is Bob and I am a writer"

"So fucking what, does that make you something?"
He turned his head in the direction of the voice and right around the corner walking along the ledge came Henry Miller – he was in a worn-out suit, bald, round glasses, young, maybe 40 or 42, he sat right down beside him and pulled out a bottle of wine, took a deep pull laid his head back and closed his eyes – then he opened them and started laughing,

"Wonderful" he said "Just wonderful"

"I thought you of all people would agree with me" said Bob -

"Didn't say I didn't…but what makes someone interesting, think about it" And there was that beautiful Brooklyn scrawl,

"I don't know, don't find many people interesting"

"Usually, when one finds themselves bored, bored with people, with things and places, the boredom is within themselves, dontcha know?"

"How did you do it, Henry, what kept you so interested for so long?"

"Life is wonderful, as long as there is health, there is endless beauty – pass the wine, if you please" He took a long pull -

Bob looked at the city skyline stretching as far as the eye could see familiar buildings screaming into the night, there was the City-Lights building with blue neon dancing up-top chimney stack reaching for the heavens, and the Artspace building down low where he rented a room once to rehearse a play he had written which never got made, just to the right the Bank of Montreal grinning its evil money-shit in the face of all that's holy, and the Sportscentre where he saw the Chicago Bulls play in all the glory-days and glory-nights got drunk that night and the night after and the night after that –

Henry sighed, then chuckled, then laughed outright patting Bob on the shoulder and passing the wine –

"It's not that I believe humanity is going to get better" Said Henry "the world and our civilization is doomed, of that I have no doubt"

"Then what's the fucking point?"

"Even though the world is busy flushing itself down the toilet, there is always time to sing and dance – you owe it to yourself – and to them"

"Them?"

"The gods, of course"

Then he laughed and laughed....

Bob laughed too but the laughter died quickly – he looked at Henry and smiled sadly....a sparrow sang something awful then settled on the ledge beside him and just sat there, alive, purposeful and full of meaning – Bob stared at it and saw all the beauty that had eluded him his entire life and all the bullshit he had done, all the harm and ugliness, all the people that had crawled through his world full of mean and spite and absolute stupidity, and the sparrow looked back and grinned – Bob's eyes filled with water but no tears fell and he looked back at Henry who was staring intently with sadness and feeling,

"It all seems so ugly" Said Bob –

"I know...I know...."

And then there was silence...and the silence was murder...and it was beautiful....then a cop car ran the streets and the sirens howled and painted everything red and blue – and someone screamed – and someone laughed – and the lights of the world went velvet blue and shone so bright it hurt –

"You see?" Said Henry smiling "You see?"

Bob looked at the city and said nothing –

"Did I ever tell you of the time me and Anais went to see Django Reinhardt play at a gypsy camp just outside Paris?"

"Anais? Nin - ?" Said Bob,

"The one and only – you know who Django Reinhardt is?"

"Yeah, sure – the greatest guitar player of all time, they say"

"And a first class hell-raiser, dontcha know"

"You three could get into some trouble"

"He was supposed to play a concert, at a hall, you know, but instead, he ran away just before the show and came to this gypsy camp he had frequented his entire life, I understand…he was always doing this type of thing apparently…Anais was at my apartment in Place Clichy, we were drinking wine and had just finished fucking…"

"-Fucking Anais Nin…"

"We heard about the show from my friend, Osborne, who in turn had been fucking a young girl that worked at the concert hall, and she had told him that Django had taken off, you know, disappeared, just before his show…my first novel had recently been published, Tropic of Cancer…"

"Wow…"

"Django, apparently, had read it and was a fan of mine and he had told Osborne, who he knew through the young girl, to tell me to go to this particular gypsy camp on the outskirts of the city, of Paris…well, we went as soon as we heard, of course, you'd be a complete moron not to. It turned out to be one of the most wonderful nights I can remember – the music was superb – the food and wine, well, was everywhere, there were beautiful women, beautiful gypsy women that were free, dontcha know, and happy and drunk, the light of the world was bright in their eyes, and we smoked opium inside trailer camps full of hard-looking characters that you knew had seen a bullet or two – yet they were friendly, and cultured it seemed, in a savage but intelligent way, so we danced, and we listened, and we drank, and we fucked and it seemed Anais and I would never, could never, split up….but of course, we did…"

And there came that silence again as Mr. Miller put his head down, briefly -

"But you know – even in that moment of sadness, when Anais finally – well, when it had become clear that we were not going to be together anymore, romantically, sexually, even intellectually, when it felt like the world and time itself was ending, I knew that even this, in some way, was beautiful, dontcha know?"

"And what was Django like?" Said Bob taking wine gulps then passing the bottle to Henry,

"– full of life bastard such as I have never seen before – I loved him - he died young, you know…."

Bob looked down 18 stories to the street saw a young lady whistling herself into oblivion, saw a drunk man flexing big brother muscle and feeling no pain, saw young Kid Bucky take it in the guts, saw Sister Lucy rape her way to the top, saw Johnny B. plant a kitchen knife right into her forehead, saw a goddamn giant piece of shit hit the pavement and explode, then he looked to his left, to his right, up then down, then saw his good friend Henry Miller...

"You were always my favorite" Said Bob,

"Wasn't I everyone's?"

They laughed, man, did they laugh –

"Well, I'm probably going to a better place anyway..." Said Bob –

"For all you know, kid, the only place you are going is straight down to the pavement"

"I had a night like that, like you just described – without the celebrities though..."

"Go on..."

"It was at an alternative rock bar, right when that Alt music was exploding in the early 80's – great time for music, man...y'see, on the surface, music was horrible, but underground all this cool shit was happening...."

"I wouldn't know, I was already dead...."

"It was a band called *Me, Mom and Morgentaler*, a Canadian band, I think...me and my friends were partying as usual, smoking pot, drinking – I was somewhere in my twenties, still single, still happy...trying to be a writer...I don't remember when we first noticed each other, but I do remember that when we did, we couldn't stay apart...we danced and talked and drank all night man...both our group of friends just disappeared to us, it was her and me, that's all....looking into each other's eyes like the secret to existence was there, a complete and total connection, right down to the soul....and always that great music roaring away, making us scream into each other's ears, laughing, our lips touching...."

"Wonderful, just wonderful!"

"We were only together for about six or seven months, off and on, but her face is the one that sticks out most in my mind...her face on that first night, the way she smiled at me and flirted...the way we loved each other immediately....her name was Claudia...what an experience, it was something else, man...

"That alone should tell you something, kid..."

The sadness fell down and around Bob as the sirens, once again, painted the night red...a gust of wind blew his hair across his face and he smelled gasoline and chemicals and vitriol and shot-gun-madness, he looked at Henry - there were tears in his eyes but they did not fall,

"Always bright and merry..." Said Henry,

He turned away, breathed in hard and heavy, looked back, and Henry Miller was gone...

The city was alive with sound all black and purple and red and tragically alluring full of everything he was, golden and rotten...he looked down, unsure for a second, sad, happy...happy, sad -

And then there was silence...and the silence was murder...and it was beautiful....

# LADY MICHELLE

And the wild dogs howled in the night, and the dead-end vultures circled endlessly, and that blue-sky-mining touched you on the shoulder and shouted YELP, and that slide-guitar in your nightmares made a craaaaaazy sound like Beelzebub in red heels salivating at the end of your bed, but yeah, Michelle was a hooker….I worked the night shift at a high rise in the ghetto security guard with no clue whatsoever as to the actual reality of things, hell, only took the job cuz I thought it would be quiet and I would be left alone to smoke my pot and wander the hallways and the outside grounds, alone is what I wanted, yeah, I wanted to be left alone…well, I wasn't a miserable recluse seeing myself superior or anything like that, didn't mind the company of people while having drinks socializing at the local pub, but when sober, when working, when going through the endless routines of life, I needed to face that immeasurable misery alone…

So there I was – a security guard, or better, a night watchman – broke, living paycheck to paycheck, selling some weed on the side just to make ends meet, you know…turned out to be a horror of a place full of nothing but trouble man, but I did manage to get high alone and with tenants and co-workers and visitors and whatever the hell cuz in those places you have the ugly and the beautiful too, and I met Michelle just like that – on night off visiting some good-natured drinker or another (I lived right across the street in another ghetto high rise) she was there reading her poetry out loud at the kitchen table high on more than just pot beer in one hand cigarette in fingers crooked smile sad voice cute and strong, several artists scattered around room, musicians, painters, fringe dwelling ghetto types looking for thrills, chills and quiet violence – I was one of two writers (the other was dead-drunk wrote vampire novels that no one read as opposed to my street-writing-lyric that no one read) and dug what she was reading,

"Where did you learn to write like that?" I said

"You like it?"

"Yeah, great stuff"

She was in jean cut-offs the cut-line visible loose ends tickling the top of her thighs red hair pearl-white skin blue eyes looking young and mean and smart and far away from what she did for a living –

"Love is everything" She said

"Sure…almost everything, anyway…"

And she was very tall, 5'10", maybe 5'11", and had curves running up and down that crazy body small waist big hips and thighs she walked clumsily but confident with shoulders hunched long hair flowing and bouncing and the smoke from her cigarette all around her, down the street her favorite drinking joint we tied it on more than once at that place old men and young thugs sharing the room with working-girls pimps small-time criminals and me – hell of a place but if there be no women, there be no cry, and there be no life, and there be no sweet-moment-to-moment, we got involved somehow, and sure it was good, and sure it was tough, and sure the rain fell, but baby, the light shone just a little brighter on you...

Tough seeing her walk out the front door late at night dressed to kill with some john hanging on her arm those fishnets and red pumps casting a shadow on my mind myself pretending to ignore, pretending to feel nothing, pretending I was better than I was, keeping it all inside somewhere deep and dark – she had an easy personality for the most part but prone to crying bouts on certain occasions for specifics unknown tough and shy at the same time downright serious to jubilant laughter she was searching, do you understand? She was going somewhere unknown and exciting and goddamn scary and didn't want to get off the ride, no way, my trip a different one, one of a constant struggle with boredom and the never-ending quest to shoot it between the eyes, but no matter cuz one night in particular beginning of shift 'round midnight long hair tied back in ponytail I was sitting bored and hungover inside security office waiting for moment when I could spark a reefer one eye on the cameras and the other on the constant stream of thugs and welfare bums and junkies and gang members and hookers and drunks and general street urchins parading earnestly in and out of the front door directly to my right, let me tell ya, it was a gathering of the unwanted night-people from all over the world Africans, Filipinos, Koreans, Pakistanis, East Indians, Arabs, Americans,

Aboriginals, Germans, Croatians, Canadians, what a trip baby, inner-city in The Great White North as lousy and lovely as everywhere else – so my radio croaked, "Bzzzzzzzz, there is a noise complaint coming from apartment 2108, respond please…"

Jesus Christ, man –

"Understood, on my way" I said

So inside elevator shooting up top past all sorts of shit and laughter and droopy eyes stopping at 21st floor get out running country music blaring from somewhere down the hall, started moving thinking fucking hell ain't feeling this at all, not at all, saw open door walked inside and there she was man – name was Rosie, middle-aged Native broad always spinning on junk and pills and booze and bad love affairs, all fucked up and crying and barely aware and I bet you never heard a sound like that,

"Rosie, c'mon man, what is it this time?" I said,

"He threatened to kill me, Ziggy….really…."

"Well listen, Rosie…"

"He just got out of jail for rape, you understand me?"

"Okay, ummm…"

"He's hurt…children….he's a murderer"

As she said the last word and I raised my arms in defiance the door behind flew open hitting my back sending me forwards and in came this small muscular man with burns and grafted skin all over him looking outta this world fucking scary,

"Look" He said to me "I don't want any trouble man"

"THAT'S HIM, FUCK, HE'S GONNA KILL ME"! Screamed Rosie,

"Now hold it, buddy" I said moving between them,

"FUCK YOU BITCH! I JUST WANT MY RING BACK!"

I saw the big diamond on her finger she held tight while moving further behind me, they got into it screaming and cursing and threatening while I stood between them thinking that I didn't want to die on this particular night, not for something this goddamn stupid, not for people that didn't give a damn about me, not for a job that paid 10 cents over minimum wage, and that burned bastard got increasingly agitated and the threat of real violence towards my skinny underfed body suddenly became very, very real – SMASH - door flies open again hits the wall then slams shut - in comes this big fucker from down the hall – dude worked as a bouncer at an uptown bar also huge customer of mine cuz he loved the green and we had become friendly and he had heard my "concerned" voice from down the hall, and here he was – well – the burned guy saw this as an immediate threat and lunged right at my friend and seeing this I joined in trying to split them apart but Rosie added her own drama and was at my throat with those long long fingernails 3 inch fuckers ready to slice and dice she painted them different colors red, blue, purple, yellow, black, and to me at that moment they shone like death so here we were with myself against one wall holding Rosie's wrists as she slashed, dove, ripped at me, and in the middle of the room you see this little guy burned skin from head to toe trying to lift this huuuuuuuuuuuuge motherfucker off the ground from the legs, ya dig? The harder he tried the more the bouncer wrapped himself around him and they wrestled like that across the carpet, what a sight, what horror, what a drag man I really hated that job....we all just kind of got tired at the same time and we stopped....breathing hard, staring at each other, knowing nothing, knowing nothing at all...burned guy looked at me gnarly finger pointed at my forehead,

"I GOT YA DEAD IN SIGHTS, YOU FUCKING PRICK, YOU'RE A DEAD MAN!"

"Fuck you, asshole, I'm right here..." I said calmly and meaning every damn word...

He gave the bouncer the middle finger -

"Faggot" He said running out of the room with Rosie begging after him.

......................................................

Used to love how we hid our relationship from the straight tenants Michelle rubbing her body swiftly and gently against me in packed elevator could feel her tremble as our bodies touched and moved on, coming down to front lobby in the middle of the night in her jean-shorts right by security office and we talked and read her poetry and talked again, smiling, vibrating, feeling right and real, we would meet at one apartment or another as friends invited us in after midnight and our relationship became known to the night-people of the building but everybody cool and easy, and we would smoke some pot and hang out with tenants in quiet apartments Iggy And The Stooges playing in the background not so loud, not so crazy, and it felt right on, like it could never end, like the jazz and rock and roll and our untouchable youth was there to stay — and one night round 5 AM there were a few of us up in 1803 and the party was moving had my security tie on radio by my side, artist friend called Leo there, welfare guitarist called Linda purring on the sidelines, few other unwanted party-souls slipping and sliding and feeling great and for a moment I thought what a cool job this is to get paid for this level of slacking, this level of fun and life-loving movement sailing the dark seas in the big cities of the lost world and the evil all around,

"How are you, Leo?" I said,

"Hey, check this out, my latest painting..."

There it was about 3 feet by 5 acrylic on canvas beautiful rendition of Aboriginal spirituality river winding its way out of sight thick forest on either side loons on the water and the face of a Native chief in full headdress in the sky blending into a wave of orange/red,

"Good work man, I dig it"

"600 bucks, want it?"

"That's funny man, where the hell would I get that kind of cash..."

He laughed, loud, genuine, drunk, two front teeth missing big gut batman t-shirt our 2 year friendship had become close and closer and he was all-street and all-tough but he could talk the good talk, he could speak art, film and books for hours on end and had an innate wisdom that you can't teach in school baby,

"Are you still an atheist?" He said

"I was never an atheist...just don't like religion..."

"But..."

Linda started dancing to an old Hoodoo Gurus song, "Turn On", right in the middle of the living room then Michelle joined in and I started on the whiskey( but slow and easy) music laying down that beautiful back-tap and I felt so goddamn fine, do you know what I am saying? Have you experienced this all-out beauty, this encompassing blue and grey and easy sensation – everything is good – everything is right – everything is as it should be – have you felt this dear reader? Then 7 AM came along and I was officially off the clock threw my tie off and we were wasted, no bullshit, but there wasn't a shred of ugly, not even a bit….Michelle looked at me while the rock and roll played on our eyes telling each other everything and we would touch our foreheads and kiss and talk and squint in the early morning drunken sunlight streaming through the slanted windows working class rabble dragging their corpses out of bed hitting the streets and beginning their last-mile walkabout, my sweet Lady Michelle - her laughter and tears running through my mind angry and sensitive personality a beacon of lost beauty, then one night – one night few years after we had stopped seeing each other and I was far removed from that job, that place, that world, she was found dead, strangled, under a bed in a seedy downtown fleabag hotel that I had drank at many, many times – made the front page of the paper and I read it while drinking coffee to keep my love for that early morning beer buzz at a safe distance – there she was - glowing like heaven large smile looking into the camera, looking right at me, looking as happy as she used to get, so full of light and promise and absolute honest care and concern for the world – that was it – she was gone – she wasn't coming back – her poetry forever unknown, her lovely madness unknown, her heavy metal gossamer unknown, and the rest of this gutter-world keeps moving forward at light speed, up on its hind legs and stumbling into the rotten alley, blinding bright, beautiful, terrible, and doomed…

But my Lady Michelle walked its narrow streets and broken down pathways once long ago - and I with her….

# SLAM-DUNK WITH A HEAVY CRUCIFIX

Somewhere around halfway through the 3rd quarter I realized just how shitty I was...we were down 13 points and I was doing nothing to change that though I was working my ass off hitting the boards and balling the rebounds but I was sissy, too damn slow getting outmuscled and outhustled and that goddamn awful crowed roared and howled and cheered and spat out the worst fucking shit-obscenities man oh man it was brutal and I had grown to hate every second of it...funny when I think that I used to live for it, there was nothing but basketball man, growing up in Australia reaching 7 feet what the hell else could I do, run away with the fucking circus? Got scouted by the NBA during an international friendly and the next thing you know I was living in the USA small-time millionaire and by sheer luck and bullshit grace I was on a team with a superstar, actually THE SUPERSTAR, and suddenly we won - not one championship, not two championships, but three in a row! Can you believe that shit man? Only been done two other times in the history of the NBA I was thinking, but right at that moment "he" stole the ball and flew down the court weaving side to side right by and through their entire team and dunked that goddamned rock nice and hard, man, nice and hard. Of course the crowd went fucking ballistic – I'm telling ya, that guy could fly, at 33, he could still fly like his shit didn't stink….it was his great comeback, the greatest comeback in sports history, they said, fucking Superman's in the building – well fuck him, I thought.

The opposition regrouped moving forward like lightning they were young, a lot younger than us, point guard shuffled and shook and threw it to the shooting guard who faced off with our shooting guard, you guessed it, Superman – another steal, what was it with that guy anyway? Once again we moved forward relentlessly the years of experience urging us on as we slowed the game to our pace – defense, when you're too old and can't run, you tighten up the game and play defense, I muscled my way in and took position under the basket, that's what Centers do, right? Superman dribbled from one side to the other, paused, pivoted, looked the other way and bulleted the no-look pass right at me, man, I caught it, fumbled, struggled, lost it and watched that motherfucker who had ripped it right out of my hands make the court and dunk like the gods had made everything in this world just for him….we were now down 15 points…our coach called a time out. As we walked to the bench I felt a sharp pain run through my balls and I tried avoiding our coach by moving far to the other side but he made a straight line for me – shit….

"Now what the fuck, exactly what the fuck are you doing out there?"

"Coach, I'm trying, that bastard keeps grabbing my balls when we get under the basket"

"Then grab his, you waste of space! How many times have I told you, stay awake till the last second, wait for that last second pass? HOW MANY TIMES, DICKHEAD?"

"That wasn't the play you called for! He was supposed to pass to Trayvon at the point!"

"Supposed to? WHAT THE FUCK MAKES YOU THINK ANYTHING IS 'SUPPOSED' TO HAPPEN?"

"C'mon man…"

"You're a fucking child, only a child would reason like that, do you REALIZE IT?"

The assistant coach ran up, "Five seconds left"

"Sit down, fuckhead!" Said the coach. He was talking to me. "Hey Big Bill, it's your turn."

Big Bill got up, smiled at me, ran on the court, he was the backup Centre and smelt the starter position, asshole, I thought, Superman walked by looking right in my face, "Faggot" he said.

I sat on the bench someone passed me a towel and a bottle of water, fuck you, I told them…


I sat out the rest of the quarter and we were doing no better, our opponent was fantastic, best record in the league and Big Bill was playing like shit, worse than me…Superman was nothing short of phenomenal, of course, 47 points and not a bead of sweat on his beautiful African body, Jesus Christ, give me a break....truth be told we wouldn't even have been in the playoffs if it weren't for him, well hell and shit in a bowl, ain't it nice? Thinking 'bout my childhood sitting on that bench wondering what the fuck I was doing there anyway, all those early years in those Perth slums, how did this happen? Life takes us along for a ride choosing this street and that and there ain't nothing we can do, ain't no use boy, man oh man my hangover was kicking in something fierce and I just wanted to ride that bench 'till the end of the game and go home to a nice cold beer but the whistle sounded, everything stopped, and the coach looked at me, pointed a finger towards the court....

I stood face to face with my opposite on their team, a superstar in his own right, as the ref through the ball up, I paused, let him have a go of it, muscled my way up, tipped the ball backwards, he gave me the finger, Superman flew right by us ball in hand like it was fucking glued there, we set up our triangle offence and I did my thing under the basket, I could still taste last night's booze and it encouraged me somehow, their point guard taunted me talking shit about my mother, fuck you midget, I said! Superman dribbled his way into position, paused, rose high up into the air, and let that jump shot fly...oooooooooooooooohh went the crowd...the ball hit the rim and bounced...I was right underneath it...I went for it, big smile on my face, confident, proud...at the same time Superman flew high above all of us, collided with me, dunked it hard, we hit the ground Superman on top of me his crotch in my face...he stayed there for a second, wiggled it around some, then got up...the basket counted and some idiot had fouled him as well...the crowd was deafening...Superman smiled, went to the foul line and got ready for the three point play, I got your number, I thought, I got your number...

Closing in on the last 7 minutes of the game I got into an altercation with their superstar Centre as he shoved me into the photographers courtside, I fell back, tripped, landed on  one of them and that fucker got ejected, crowd was on their feet chanting my name, yeah, I thought, that's it...Superman came up to me and extended his hand...I took it...

We had 6 minutes to get rid of a 12 point deficit and I felt damn confident, we moved the ball smoothly from one guy to the next methodically making our way to the paint, that's the way old guys played, mathematically, 2 plus 2 equals 4, I stood a few steps away from the basket this time but close enough to make the kill, my teammates set it up, they looked like African gods, so smooth, so lithe, Superman brought the ball up, why not, and he was doing his thing, I felt my asshole rumble, he faked, dribbled, stopped dead, threw it my way, I shifted, muscled my way in front of the basket, farted, grabbed the ball and made the kill... ref waved it off as the crowd booed his ass right out of town...illegal defense, he said, before the basket...illegal defense? After all these years of playing the game I still didn't know what that meant, don't think anyone really did...so we got over that and tried again, ball came my way, I hung on, faced my opponent, faked, triple-pumped, and dunked that bastard hard! Again, the crowd chanted my name...I felt the hairs on the back of my neck stand up straight...I looked over at Superman as I ran down the court...he winked and pointed a finger at me approvingly....I couldn't help but smile...they made their run, angry, and stunned us with a 3 pointer...those fuckheads were good...the linesman passed me the ball as I stood on our baseline, I passed it to Superman and we resumed play with him running up the court and encouraging me, I followed him while blowing wind, spotted a young blonde in the front row, short skirt, big thighs, screaming out my name, then I saw our coach, he was screaming out my name as well but in a decidedly different tone, 3 point arc coming up fast, I stepped over it, ran to the basket, Superman still had the ball, he dribbled back and forth at the point trying to find an opening but they had us covered to the man, for a second I thought of a Vonnegut novel I had read in high school, then I saw our boys scrambling panic on their faces 24 second clock winding down, 12, 11, 10, Superman dribbled side to side, 8, 7, 6, I turned to my left trying to find an opening but their guy was right in my face, the boys started running but they had us, my eyes met with Superman's, he smiled, shifted into gear, sliced through the trap, hit the paint, their defense closed in huddling under the basket, and that's when he took off, ball in hand, fucking rocket on his back, high above everyone, and I ran to the middle as our boys scattered, as the crowd held their breath, as the nuclear missiles lay dormant, as the volcanoes burped, as I watched him soar over everything I had ever held sacred, and he hung there, and he smiled, and my hangover was in remission, and we all just stood there waiting for him to come down, lit a few smokes, had a chat, thought about this and that, and the inner-city court was far behind me and I never hated Superman as much as I did then...

# SWEET SHIVER BURN

Gassino was its name, Italian village on the outskirts of the northern city called Torino and it was in the foothills of the Italian Alps built on a slope stretching up and up to the top of the town where old villas sat facing the village below lights twinkling like fireflies at night looking for love, sex, vengeance – mountains loomed over everything tall and majestic clouds like gentle explosions framing their peaks just outside my backyard you felt like you could touch them, like you could spit on all their holy bullshit and the hell with the lot of them, when you're fixing to die it all comes together anyway, all to an end and everything in the end and to the beginning and back again, I lived there in one of those villas, a particularly modern one built out of orange bricks and just about the size of a small school, fucking big thing man, but welcoming and warm and always full of people lit up like firecrackers fixing to die...

Mother there, grandmother, great-grandmother, father and brother back in Canada, myself a kid of 14 just coming into puberty and digging all the young Italian chicks walking around the village and trekking up to the mountains right by the path in front of my house, all this beautiful rendering of flesh and youthful desire some kind of torturous heaven for a kid my age…from my place the journey to the village was all downhill a twisting narrow road lined with small stone houses and cafes on both sides me hugging the walls as cars raced by without a thought or care about my ass, and I would ride my bike down those streets hitting speeds dangerous to body and soul and thinking back I realize my damn luck cuz the road was so steep, y'see, that hitting the brakes was impossible – you started at the top of the road, took the plunge, and until you hit the flat land of the village center you were at the mercy of the gods and of those fuckheads driving those cursed Fiats like there was absolutely no time to waste, not a second to spare, life is short, yes it is, feeling the wind of cars as they barely miss you, feeling the rush and the fear of near-death, and the graceful radiant luck as you skid to a halt at the mouth of the village….

Went flying over handlebars and smashed right into a fence once, car tire racing by my head as I lay on the ground wondering if God loves me….stopped taking the bike after that…but those jaunts to the town center were full of problem-free joy and if you have ever been to Italy then you understand what I mean when I describe that smell of cooking always present, that life-affirming aroma that hangs in the air like the solution to everything, especially pervasive in the small villages that dot the entire country and that are the real Italy, but no matter, the butcher's shop and that strange looking woman hanging on the front stoop as a thin trickle of blood flowed to the street, the café with the old men playing cards and drinking espresso and brandy day and night arguing about soccer, politics, life, the bread shop – man, the bread shop – you want to talk about diggin' it? Is there a better aroma than baking bread? All kinds of bread, flat bread, long bread, sourdough, pane Toscano, French baguette, panini, pancarre, I would stop there every day after school and just hang out for a while, just smile and dig being alive, what ever happened to that feeling?

Then there was the outdoor swimming pool just a few blocks from my school, used to go with my friends and cousins during summer break and we awkwardly flirted with the girls our age and dug their bathing suits and their mischievous smiles and their need to play the game, and all the village young people on a Saturday afternoon feeling like this was everything, there was nothing else, and if there was, we couldn't have cared less – this was the entire world, and it was fine, and it was enough – one of the lifeguards was a woman, maybe 21 or 22 years old, and she was my first crush, my first older woman, I never spoke to her of course, never even smiled at her, it was enough to look at her in her black bikini, red bikini, purple bikini, gold bikini with black dots, thick brown hair curly and wild, tan skin and painted toes and thighs as round as heaven, and it was enough to think of her when I was alone at home hand in my pants all my fantasies as real as anything and in my 14 year old head she was there, sitting right beside me in my room as we discovered rock and roll, as we listened to old April

Wine records and wondered and marveled at this new music-thing suddenly in our lives…

Rock and roll made me feel like the truth was at hand's reach loud and sloppy, my first and truest love causing an explosion in my life beyond description, all that guitar riffing and fuzzing tearing the skies wide open, those drums banging the shit out of all things decent and holy my head snapping back and forth like war-time Ohio and Alan Freed sweating buckets spinning Little Richard records with no time left….and the walk uphill as I went home sun just kind of hanging low waiting to disappear, took the opposite way many times up an open road large field on either side town cemetery bright and lonely I would stop there…great-grandmother's grave rest my back against tombstone and think – about her, about me, about my school, about Canada I left behind, about father and brother in Canada, about doing something stupid and crazy, but enough with it, I would slowly make for home my young knees feeling no pain walking the steep slope road turning to gravel then through the woods past the wild dogs and even wilder cats, took great-grandmother there for a walk once – she was about 84 years old, very short, chubby, big nose, kerchief on her head, but in incredible shape and endurance like those old-village people are without even trying and felt mischievous started telling her all sorts of stories about bandits in the hills, and wild animals roaming the countryside, and the bandits would kidnap people and hold them for ransom, great-nonna beginning to get scared hanging on to me tight yet enjoying the trip, I could tell, she knew I was bullshitting but the thrill was like riding a rollercoaster, y'now, a safe kind of scare….

So 45 minutes after leaving the swimming pool I would reach the beginning of my street gravel road leading right up to our house on the corner heard my dogs barking then saw them at the fence causing all sorts of shit, German Sheppard, Collie, Chihuahua all excited to see me, front gate green with long cement stairs leading up to an archway and there sat my great-nonna her thick grey hair in a bun peeling potatoes or mixing salads or playing solitaire, I walk in and she hugs me then gives me shit about something, mother and grandma cleaning or visiting with aunts and uncles, uh-huh…our backyard about the size of a soccer field but on a slope except for the flat stone patio grand and large that circled the house and there I went to kick the ball around dreaming of being a professional soccer player for Torino in Serie A all those fat-ass lazy fans cheering for me and me fucking around with the groupies, what a life, huh, I didn't stop until I heard my mother screaming it was suppertime and there came those Italian scents, there came that food and that way of living but just before I go in I see something through the slats of our fence neighbor's villa being right there…I see the daughter girl my age called Fiorenza sun-bathing in her red bikini and I watch in silence and I feel like the sun is melting and I feel hidden and brave and she lifts a thigh to the sky, yawns, turns her head in my direction….she sees me….she frowns….then she smiles and winks and closes her eyes…

# THE BOY, THE GIRL, THE FLOWERPOT IN THE SKYWAY

It wasn't so much the people he worked with that he hated, it was people in general – he went through all the proper motions, all the expected pleasantries, but still it came out all wrong. Nor did people like him. He didn't bring out hatred in them, just a sort of disinterest, a boredom of types. Which he returned in abundance. He liked the girls, liked their legs, their clothes, their minds, but could not muster the courage, the desire to actually interact with them. Still, they were more interesting than the boys. He often wondered how different they would feel if they actually knew him, if they saw how sensitive he was, if they saw that he was more like them. And what if they knew that he wrote poetry at night, beautiful, haunting street poems that any editor would kill to publish, but that he kept hidden as a punishment for the stupidity in the world.

Yet, there was one girl, yes, there was one.

He finished his shift as a dishwasher at 11:30 every night and walked through the shivering, concrete streets to his house. He passed broken down apartments, small cracked houses with cluttered front yards, and all sorts of street characters hanging out on corners no matter what the temperature – sometimes he bought shit from them, sometimes he didn't. But he noticed the night lights, the way everyone hovered around them, and went home and wrote about it.

He reached his house – a small one story shack of a place with two bedrooms, a washroom, living room and a kitchen. Not much to look at it but he kept it clean – his mother lived with him. She was old and could no longer live alone, not terminally sick, just too damn old. She owned the house. He was born there, raised there, and might even die there.

She sat in her usual chair watching television.

"Hi mom. How are you?"

"I am okay…how was work?"

"Well…the same…just…the same"

She stood up and hobbled her way towards him then kissed him on the cheek.

"That's all we can expect my son, there really isn't much else"

"I know, I know…"

"You are my little boy and always will be."

Then she went to her bedroom, turned the small television at the foot of the bed on, and closed the door. She did this on purpose knowing her son needed to write and to be alone. They loved each other, no bad feelings, no assignment of blame, no remorse – just a sort of loneliness that exists when you do one thing, and one thing only, for too damn long. Better than the outside world, he thought.

He wrote for a while then started thinking of "her", then he wrote some more, then opened the whiskey – Rye and Coke – he continued with her in his mind until the end of the bottle, then wrote a few more poems. Thinking it had been a good night, he went to bed drunk and happy.


Morning after – he walked the many skyways of the city that connected the entire downtown as he did every day. He was one of those guys that did not get hangovers, lucky bastard. Outside the wind blew and the winter chill grasped at the side of the buildings and if you got close enough to the windows, you could feel it on your skin. The skyways were everywhere and from everywhere in the downtown area you could see the people inside walking back and forth. Endlessly, it seemed. He was hovering around the beginning of the inner-city slowly making his way through the first skyway. He tried to remain invisible while inspecting everything around him, like writers do.

And, always, an eye out for her.

There were bums and business-people and restaurant workers and janitors and window washers and drug dealers and in every single skyway there were musicians strumming their guitars and playing their harmonicas and signing their songs just hoping that something, anything, would change. But every day they were there, in the same spot, playing the same old tunes, and sometimes he dropped some change, and sometimes he didn't. He liked them, he thought they colored the world and wished he was one of them. The sad songs of the world are beautiful he thought, so beautiful. He stopped at a particular set of windows that faced the main artery of the city cutting it in half - on one side skyscrapers lined the streets and people filled the sidewalks, and on the other the buildings tapered off and a line of old, barfly hotels ran its length with the public library at the end. He thought it was a strange sight to see the street change so suddenly and dramatically, but didn't really give a shit. There was a slight widening with a bench in a corner against a wall and a couple of young dudes stood there talking. He sat on the bench and cocked his ear while pretending not to.

"Look, I don't give a fuck, we got to get the money" said 1st dude. "I want to go to that concert, man, I ain't missin' it."

"I know, I know, man." 2nd dude, "Cracker owes us some shit, maybe we can collect..."

"And what the fuck we goin' to do with some shit?"

"We sell it, asshole, then we got money"

"The concert is tonight, jackass, we goin' to sell it in that time?"

"Sure we can, we'll sell it right at the concert...man, 'That Petrol Emotion', they're my favorite band..."

"One way or another we are goin', believe THAT, dude!"

"What's your favorite record from them?"

"I like 'Chemicrazy', man, that shit is fucking awesome!"

"My favorite is 'Babble'"

"Too alternative… 'Chemicrazy' rocks more"

"They're supposed to be alternative, dude, uhh, they're an 'alternative rock' band, ya dig?"

'I get it, but 'Chemicrazy' IS alternative, just not TOO alternative – 'Babble' is hard to get into, it's fucking weird, ya know?"

"You're full of it, dude, Babble is the shit!"

'Fuck Babble….I don't need Babble…"

"But 'Swamp' is their fucking best song, man!"

"You bet, fucking rocks!"

"Lookit that chick, whew, lookit that ass baby!"

"Don't act like a jackass, dude – wow, what an ass!"

And that ass belonged to "her" – he got off the bench and followed her discreetly and watched her move through the skyways so slowly and leisurely and happy. She seemed to be interested in everything, stopping and listening and staring out windows. Even though she was dressed in office clothes and obviously on a work break, she never seemed in a hurry. But what he liked most of all, was that she was always alone. Her long curly brown hair swung from side to side and her red blouse hung loosely over her frame. She was 10 or 15 pounds overweight with olive skin and a very pretty face. She wore skirts of different colors every day, occasionally dress pants. One day, and one day only, he saw her in jeans and almost had an anxiety attack. Their eyes had never met and she was completely unaware of him. And this too, he thought, was right.

Towards the end of the downtown skyways, the hallway turned suddenly and faced an entire wall of windows on one side, and pictures of famous musicians in concert on the other. Out the windows was the view of a back alley, scarred, broken, trash bins overflowing and garbage strewn all over the street. Her pace slowed to a crawl as she studied the musicians on the wall – Lady Gaga stood there caught in one of her usual ridiculous poses – Garth Brooks faced a microphone and smiled – The Tragically Hip stood side by side in rock and roll poses guitars wailing – Stevie Knicks looked down and spread her wings – Gene Simmons moved forward with his tongue out looking for attention as always, Peter Criss eyeing him suspiciously from behind his drum set – And That Petrol Emotion did everything differently.

And here it was. Once again. The spot. At the end of the hallway, a middle aged fellow painted at an easel. The grey light and cloudy sky from outside came in from the windows and hung all around him. He was there every day. And every day she stayed there and she watched him paint. On this day, he was working on a flowerpot, from memory. The flowers were white with yellow coming from somewhere inside. The vase was red and purple and blue and green and every other color you can imagine. He had been working on it for a very long time. He wore blue-jean coveralls and had the friendliest smile in the world. She sat on the windowsill and watched. Sometimes looking sad, sometimes looking happy. Today, she looked a bit of both.

He watched from a safe distance and the fantasies, friendly, well-meaning, but full of unrequited love and white/light, white heat, went running through his head. She was oblivious to him and to everything but the flowerpot in the skyway. And this is what made it special. Everyone disappeared. The world froze. There was no sound, no movement. Only the brushes on the canvas, the middle-aged painter's smile, the boy and the girl.

And in an adjacent office building at that very moment a cleaning lady named Lillianna vacuumed the floor of an empty room. She had immigrated to Canada three years prior from Croatia. She missed her home. She turned off the vacuum and sat down. Looking out the window she saw the skyway barely 50 feet away. Through the glass she saw a young woman watching a street-painter in blue-jean coveralls at his easel. Several yards down the hall there was a young man standing still looking in the opposite direction. There was no one else in the skyway. Lillianna watched for a while and wondered what those people were about, what the story was.

Then she saw the young woman suddenly turn and look at the young man. They stood facing each other. They stood there without moving. The painter continued.

Hmmm, she thought, who cares - vacuum back on, Lillianna continued with her day...

# MINNEAPOLIS

Landed in Minneapolis on Thanksgiving middle of the afternoon -20 degrees ice-wind tearing at your face and we were there for a book signing had just released one each, my wife Izzy a book of short stories and poetry, myself a 1st person novel with long passages of stream of consciousness spontaneous prose and what I called WORD MUSIC….we were indie writers publishing our own shit and giving nothing but disdain to the mainstream publishing world, not cuz we were assholes, but cuz - well, they sucked - year after year of rejection letters from publishing houses that I never wanted to be published from in the first place and laughing long and loud upon reading these miserable apologies – *we love your writing BUT* – so there we were – the U.S. – coming from Winnipeg happy sad and just a little pissed off….we were also there for another reason – on the same night as our signing Bob Dylan was playing at the Target Centre AND it was Izzy's 40th birthday – this being an incredible confluence of events seeing that Dylan was

Izzy's favorite musician and one of her favorite poets, weird shit, let me tell ya…

They're similar the two cities, Winnipeg and Minneapolis, same weather, literary, arty, great music scene, working class, high crime, lots of downtown bums, long hot summers, and always, always struggling – exactly what an artist needs the hell with sun and water and beaches and trendy nightspots and travels across the world and Paris and London and Milan and New York and The Caribbean and we hopped in the shuttle in route to our hotel, damn thing full of straight assholes talking 'bout thanksgiving and family and it's alright man, ain't raggin' on everyone and everything, we got a family, we hang out on holidays, we dig the people in our life to no end, but must there always be this all-present family component? Can we not escape from time to time? Can we not simply be individuals?

After all that phony shit, "yes, happy thanksgiving", "yes, to you and your family", "yes, we love the U.S.", "Yes, Canada is great too", and on and on, we pulled up in front of our hotel, tipped the driver, walked into a pretty posh place, we had booked the plane tickets and hotel as a package didn't even realize what we were getting, didn't give a shit if it was rich or poor and it turned out to be somewhere in-between right downtown across from the Target Centre where The Minnesota Timberwolves played basketball (dig it, baby) and where Mr. Tambourine Man himself would be showing us his stuff, Izzy all tough and coooool looking round lobby feeling her return to her home country in full bloom and viewing it with some suspicion but loving it as well as the devil may care and god may not, but we were alive and together and ready….

"Let's put our bags away and let's find something to do, what do you say?" Said Izzy,

"Sounds good to me man, let's hurry" I said,

"Lookit this room, what do you think?"

"Pretty small, pretty cool…nothing wrong with it…big T.V.…."

"Wow, I must admit, I'm a bit excited"

"That is the best way to go through life"

"I can't believe we're going to see him live, I can't fucking believe it!"

"And we're signing books and all that shit…"

"I hear ya…but let's not talk about the book signing"

"Why not…I mean, that's why we're here, right?"

"I was thinking we'd give it a break for a while, huh?"

"Alright, baby, you ready to hit the American streets?"

The thing about Izzy is that her face body and everything about her was incredibly expressive, never a moment of passivity, never a flat uninterested look, she could be shy and a bit withdrawn in a group but the second she was engaged her face lit up like a carnival in full-blown motion, she was tall and curvy and wild and kind and wrote like Lucifer was on her ass, born and raised in America damn proud of it but also damn critical of it she walked beside me down 1st Avenue up to Hennepin and the tall buildings and the theatres and skyways connecting the whole damn thing…streets were empty and the bars were closed and what the fuck did we think, it was thanksgiving and people cared about this shit, especially in the U.S., and it was damn cold wind blowing at our faces tearing at our skin just like in Winnipeg, wow, so I said,

"Alright, Izzy, this sucks, let's go back to the hotel and get drunk…"

"Do we have anything, I don't remember…"

"Got a big-ass botte of Rye I brought from home…we'll be hungover for the signing though…"

"Who cares, we're Canadian, fuck 'em…"

"But you're American, baby"

"Not for this week, let's hurry, I can't feel my fucking face"

We got lost along the way and with the freezing wind nipping at our heels we thought this was the end circling and grooving in and out of the skyscrapers till we found a poor fucker down on his luck and asked him where the hell we were and where the hell was our hotel, he told us, we flipped him a few bucks and ran our asses down the street…there was a swanky bar on the 5th floor not really our style but as long as the assholes left us alone and no one wanted to get in a fist fight just cuz his life had been a sorry mess we could drink anywhere, so we stopped there on the way to our room skin red and frozen and our breath still coming out in clouds and people looking at us like we didn't belong cuz I had long hair and was scruffy and Izzy looked all indie and rock-and-roll Annie Hall, but, as I said, this bothered us none – hmmm, Rye and 7 for me, Rye and 7 for Izzy, smiles and grins, faces thawing, fingers gnarly, bartender slick and well-groomed, people dressed like money, few drinks down our starving gullets and off we go – elevator up and running we're stuck in there with the rest of the losers start chatting with a guy and his gal and they are friendly and happy and we dig them booze on their breath, there we were in our room I ordered 7-up and ice and we plugged our Ipod into the station (man I missed records) with our 7000 song music collection blasting into the room we had it on random and Alex Harvey started up, and if you haven't heard Mr. Harvey's band, then you ain't lived, "Ain't nothing like a gang bang" was playing, then it switched to Joe Strummer, The Beatles, Thelonious Monk and so on, we looked out the windows facing the Minneapolis skyline and it was impressive and beautiful and full of dancing lights, much bigger than Winnipeg's, saw the sport fans gather in front of the Arena for the Timberwolves basketball game, a limousine pulled up, they were playing the Lakers and Izzy wondered if Kobe Bryant was in that limousine acting like an asshole, we kept drinking slow but steady and talked, and laughed, and kissed, and we went outside where the smokers gathered so Izzy could get her cigarette fix and met people from all over the U.S. friendliest people I've ever known don't give me no shit about Americans, one young couple had just gotten married and they had multiple rooms with friends partying and they were cool and average looking, tall lanky guy, short woman with high heels and mini-skirt, both tipsy and talking fast and interested in the fact that we were writers,

"So you're from Ohio?" Said the girl to Izzy,

"Yeah, moved to Canada 7 years ago..."

"How do you like it?"

"It's great, not that different from here at all..."

"More liberal, I'll guess"

"Politically it is...doesn't really trickle down to the street, though...it feels the same as here, very little difference"

"Minneapolis especially" I cut in, "Feels exactly like Winnipeg, they're sister cities, for sure"

"I went to Winnipeg once to see a bar-band called Propagandi" Said the guy,

"Man, I remember them!" I said,

"Oh yeah" He laughed "I loved them! Felt right at home in Winnipeg"

"So you dug it?"

"You bet"

"Man, what a day" said the girl "Both our parents are divorced so we had to go to four thanksgiving dinners, Jesus!"

Wind blowing cold but we weren't feeling it, weren't feeling nothing man –

"Good stomach coating for the drinks" I said,

Izzy laughed and cheered and put out her cigarette –

"See you guys later, congratulations! So you're coming to our signing tomorrow? Got the address?" Said Izzy –

"We will be there!" She said,

We ran into the lobby and to the elevator and were back in our room, we took our pants off and drank in our underwear, and we danced and sang to 'La Vie En Rose' from Louis Armstrong, and suddenly IN-A-GADDA-DA-VIDA blasted our reality and we got it on and stumbled and held on tight and we rolled around the bed really digging each other and I said 'nice to love you, baby' and that fuzz-box guitar went on forever and the room twisted and melted and us seeing double I swear Jesus was there smug and smiling and he passed me a joint until Izzy finally passed out all nice and lovely her face barely sticking out of the covers, I sat there for a while drinking slowly staring out windows at looming skyline, could hear people partying and howling from the room above and wondered if it was the newlyweds and their gang, put on the headphones and listened to 'Doolittle' from The Pixies beginning to end, had a few more drinks in silence, listened to 'Up To Here" by The Tragically Hip, whole album, then, seeing triple and head spinning happily and feeling that thing called 'life' in full force, crawled into bed with Izzy, hugged her, she complained and turned away, I rolled up into my head and went to sleep…

We were booked for two signings on successive nights, the first was with a group of indie writers, the other was just us – tables were set up around the room hugging the walls and  there was a row in the middle everyone with their banners and posters and books laid out and there was huge sign on the wall that said ANARCHIST BOOK FAIR, we weren't anarchists, nor did we give a shit about politics, nor had we been informed about this stuff from the bookstore – it was a small place with a rather large room on the side which was where we were and our 6 foot banner hung above us with our Indie Press name and SPONTANEOUS PROSE AND POETRY written on it, 15 titles displayed on the table, over 100 books in total…it was impressive and we couldn't help but feel proud – we had written and published all these books and seeing them laid out in front of us like that made us smile, no matter if they were bad or good or average or if anyone gave a shit, the sheer output alone showed that we were dedicated to our craft, that it wasn't just a hobby, and that we weren't just pretending….

So it began – doors were opened to the public, we all sat there staring at each other and waiting – man, I was hungover and I could tell Izzy was feeling the pain but we were veteran drinkers and ain't nothing too much for us, no one came in, I looked out the window residential neighborhood few people walking around doing nothing warm winter day -5 degrees Celsius, Izzy took a sip of coffee and furrowed her brow, our publicist had booked this thing at our cost of course and we knew nothing about the bookstore or the event or the neighborhood and didn't look it up either – we had a few months of good book sales which gave us a few extra bucks in our jeans so we said, WHAT THE FUCK, LET'S DO IT!

Not much action – I started looking around the room noticing the other writers – one table had a non-descript looking duo, man and woman, baggy t-shirts, kinda fat and boring, woman had glasses and long straight hair, few comic books on the table and they sat still barely moving small poster on floor saying, BATHTUB PRESS, other table was a group of long hairs looking like hippe-wanna-bees a family with kids in tow and organic food and a set of magazines on the table, something about organic farming and 'homespun poetry" their banner behind them read HEARTFELT PUBLISHING, Jesus, I thought, what in the hell, then came the anarchists – a group of young people hovered around each other's tables and they looked tough and bitter and they talked about politics without knowing politics and their banners read like this –

JUST SAY FUCK YOU PUBLISHING –

PEOPLE DECIDE, GOVERNMENT LIES –

Table just to the right had a middle-aged man with long hair tight t-shirt which showed off his man-breasts, his publication was about the mistreatment of women in third world countries and he sat there looking bored and smart, Izzy and I dug him, and his cause, another table had skinhead woman selling marijuana paraphernalia and magazines on the subject, and then there were a few poetry small presses, an indie distributor with a black beard long hair tied back in a ponytail and an asshole look on his face, and an artist with some paintings and a few self-published comic books, old dude bald head with grey hair around ears thin build big smile handlebar mustache…he saw us…started looking at our banner, at us, back at the banner, rubbing his chin…

"Oh oh…" I said,

"I hear ya" Said Izzy,

He came over thin tight body zig-zagging its way in and out of the tables –

"Hi guys, what's up?"

"Not much, man, how's it going?" I said,

"Hey…" Said Izzy,

"Well this is quite the set-up you have here…you'll have to explain what spontaneous prose means…"

"And what do you do?" Asked Izzy,

"I'm a painter and a comic-book artist…"

"Superheroes, or real comics?" I said,

"Ha, ha, ha, ha, ha, real comics…you familiar with Robert Crumb, The Hernandez Brothers, that kind of stuff?"

"Oh yeah, we love it…"

"It's kinda sad how superhero comics and movies have eclipsed everything…"

"Yeah, but I think that's only in the U.S. and Canada…in Europe they prefer the serious comic books, don't they?"

"I hope you're right…so tell me, what's this shit about, what do you guys write? Who publishes this stuff?"

"We publish it ourselves…it's that rebellious writing, you know, real-life stuff, no genre, no vampires, no ghosts, no super-spies, no wizards and elves and shit…"

"No zombies either, I will not tolerate zombies!" Said Izzy,

"This is an interesting style you write in" He said while flipping through one of my books,

"That's spontaneous prose and poetry, ya dig?"

"Yeah, I see, it almost looks like musical notes going down the page…I can hear the music in my head, know what I mean?"

"What's your name, pal?"

"Derrick, Derrick Friesen"

He shook our hands –

'Derrick" I said, "You may have nailed down my writing in just a few seconds"

"I like the way your sentences go on forever, it's got a natural flow you don't usually see…kinda like the Beat Writers"

"Kerouac is the only Beat Writer I like…but yeah, I know what you mean…"

Reading through Izzy's books he had the same praise,

"There's something entirely natural here…reminds me of Patti Smith's early songs…yeah, this is quite beautiful…you guys up for a trade?"

We looked at each other and decided it was cool…

"Take whatever you want, and you can give us your comic books in trade" I said,

"Sounds good…so is it entirely spontaneous, no re-writes at all?"

"Hardly any….not entirely spontaneous, it just has to "feel" spontaneous…"

"Yeah, we can't write "almost spontaneous" on our promo, know what I mean?" Said Izzy,

"Yes, I do - can I take this?" He said while holding up Izzy's first book of poems –

"Sure…" She said,

"Right on, sister, come pick a comic…"

She came back with the comic and it looked good, couple guys on the cover sitting on a curb talking about record albums, looked like something out of the 70's – then people started coming in and they paused, and they asked questions, and they moved on, scene still slow but it felt cool and rewarding as a few of the writers and publishers started talking into the mike from a small stage at the back of the room, pure nonsense, shit about publishing and how to write and the importance of editing and how to sell your books, and there were a few poetry readings that we kinda dug, Izzy especially liked a young woman that belted out a few powerful lines about love and sex and death, we clapped hard for that one, and people whistled, and our first sale happened – a young lady picked a book of mine, one of Izzy's, gave us the cash, we put it in our money box, gave her some change, smiled and congratulated each other on our first sale, good stuff baby, good stuff...


The day continued with a flow of about 10 or 20 people coming in and out every hour or so, not many of us sold much but me and Izzy and Derrick definitely sold more than the rest, and the other writers made their way to us eventually, found out some of them were professional poets (meaning they did it for a living, unlike us working shmucks) and shitty human beings to boot, as you might expect – they held us in obvious disdain and wouldn't get too near though they were always eyeballing us, a few of them even walking by snickering and I'm giving them the stare-down cuz I knew they felt threatened, cuz I knew they knew we were outselling them, sad thing being, without a word of a lie, their writing was quite bad, and Derrick agreed with us - and speaking of Derrick, every single person that stopped at his table was promptly shown Izzy's book and pointed in our direction, so we returned the favor and talked to people about writers, and cartoonists, and painters, and movies, and Canada, and the U.S. and a few more sales were made, and at a certain point the granola hippies started talking about their organic commune living and their annoying little hippie kids were running all over the place, one of the adults stood right in front of our table and talked to another guy while standing on one leg with the other bent at his side in what we found out was called The Tree Pose in Yoga, *what an asshole* whispered Izzy, his long blonde hair tied in a loose ponytail and his baggy clothes and absolutely pretentious posture making me laugh man, loud and proud and happy, and while, yes - we were bored, and yes - we would have rather been at a bar with an alternative rock band playing, or back home smoking pot and watching movies, we actually dug the whole thing leaving with a few more bucks in our jeans than when we came in...


Spent the next afternoon walking around downtown Minneapolis stopping at the Mary Tyler Moore statue on corner of 5th Street and Nicolette and Izzy posing in front of it as I took a picture, we were part of the television generation NOT the internet generation, and though we were avid readers, writers, thinkers, drinkers, we also watched a lot of television, both good and bad, and had made an enemy of the art-snob mentality that snubbed its nose at entertainment, at just getting your kicks, we had been called intellectuals by some, and we did figure North America could use an infusion of art and literature, but we were also fun-lovers, we dug our turn-ons, and that was all there was to it...let me tell ya though, Minneapolis was our type of town...there were bookstores and cafes where writers hung out, there were theatres and cinemas with old-style lightbulbs framing neon signs and pubs with Celtic music blasting out the front door, there were bums and musicians talking on street corners looking tough and mean, there were black guys asking for money in front of liquor stores and smiling and laughing as I shook their hands, there was a constant urban buzz and electricity shooting through the air, and Bob Dylan came from here, and so did The Replacements, and it was Izzy's birthday, and we cruised the warm winter afternoon taking in anything and everything and each other most of all and it was a fine and grand and beautiful moment in a beautiful North American city, ain't that something?


So on that night we were back at the book store but this time it was just us – same table and banner, same room – just us alone and a large empty space – felt weird man, and the book store employees were odd quiet types, left us in the room and sat in their separate corners, 4 of them, just hanging and reading in complete silence, not a radio playing or a word whispered – Izzy started feeling down, I could see it, and I looked at our books laid out on the table and saw how different it looked when no one else was there to see it, the night before everything feeling grand and pure, and tonight things becoming a drag real fast –

"Hey, baby" I said caressing Izzy's face "It's your birthday, and we are seeing Mr. Dylan later, no regrets, this is nothing but a blast, okay?"

"Okay" She said softly

She was my gal, ain't nothing going to ever take that away from us, and her happiness was my responsibility, and bringing it about my pleasure, and a few people came into the store, came right up to us –

"We heard your interview on the radio the other day…"

"Cool…" I said,

Izzy smiled and started talking and they were young  twenty-somethings and they bought a few books and we talked for a good half an hour and they were sunshine and laughter, right on I said as they left – I kissed Izzy and smiled, she smiled back her mood lifting and suddenly nothing but good energy coming from her and hovering above everything, and then a publisher with fedora black beard touch of grey who had also heard our radio interview came in and expressed genuine interest looking through our books smiling and obviously digging it and he talked to us for so long we figured there was a publishing contract coming our way or something big – but at the end he walked out empty handed, took our business cards and we never heard from the guy again – what the hell, it continued like that – a few people an hour came in and talked with looks on their faces that said "WOW MAN, YOU GUYS ARE THE CAT'S ASS!" yet would turn around and split without buying anything and it was starting to really bother me…I pulled out a two-liter 7-up bottle from my bag and poured a few drinks for me and Izzy…she took a sip and smiled immediately tasting the Rye…It hit my throat with some heat and went down smoothly…we managed to sell a few books but after a short time decided to fuck it – we told the bookstore people and they looked disappointed – I mentioned that I found it strange that there was so little traffic in that store, I had never seen a bookstore in Winnipeg so quiet – they said something about the fact that we were supposed to stay there all day, we said "goodbye", and got the hell out, flagged a cab, back at the hotel we showered, drank a bit, and off to see Bob we went...

And there we were...it was a packed arena and the lights went down and me and Izzy were pleasantly drunk and stoned sitting pretty damn close to the stage and here came Bob...I saw Izzy tear up a bit...I held her tight...Bob had an electric band and they tore into "All Along The Watchtower", first song...we went crazy and knew instantly it was going to be a great night...

In the end, we had lost our shirts on the Minneapolis gig...but we had sold books to strangers who had later on become fans who had turned us on to other fans and we had hung out in a cool city and we had spent Izzy's birthday watching one of the greatest musicians and poets of all time...the plane took off and Izzy put her head on my shoulder looking out the window...

"Can't wait to get home...watch some television" She said softly and tired,

"I hear ya" I said –

# SNAKE BITE

No one liked him including myself but it looked like his time may have come in hospital for weeks some kind of infection was killing him doctors didn't know shit as usual but guy didn't look good and at the end of my night shift I would go straight to the hospital and hang out for hours, talk to the guy, watch him sleep, try to make him laugh, reassure him that it would be alright...those hospital hallways so damn depressing the nurses acting like nothing was going on laughing eating texting joking with the infirm thinking this was better than just telling the truth – *you ain't doing good, pal, no sir, no sir-eeee* –

Man, I didn't know why I was visiting this guy, but I do know that hospitals make me sick and we had worked together for 5 years night watchmen in a downtown museum which he in turn had worked at for 20 years, guy was only in his late fifties ten years older than myself and as strong as shit, owned a small construction company which he sometimes worked at all day then came to the museum and toughed it out listening to loud rock and roll and always texting on that fucking ridiculous smart-phone (thought only the 20-somethings were doing this crap), but he was single, good looking older guy with a certain amount of women into him and his ways and that's where all the texts came from, he would show them off every chance he got – *hey lookit this, buddy* – some young woman's face smiling like a moron and some kind of ridiculous text trying to sound funny and sexual at the same time – *where's your women, pal? – huh?* – and that's it, he would leave it at that cuz he wasn't too bright, the sheer idiocy in this world alone was enough to make me embarrassed about being a part of the human race, and let me tell ya about the doctors – the doctors – those fucking overfed bureaucrats taking their sweet time feeling that all-important pull of the human ego at its brightest – *we're humans too, we need our coffee breaks* – like hell, if you're a doctor then you signed up for something more than "just a job", you have to be borderline superhuman in your care and concern for others and put your mighty ass second on the list, always second, do ya dig what I'm saying?

My cab pulled up to the hospital about 8:30 AM people outside smoking cigarettes some patients, some workers, some security guards, constant stream of people in and out the front doors damn huge place laid out like a maze and finding your way never easy but fine food court with some variety, that much was good, grabbed a coffee after standing in line for twenty minutes working my way through the huge crowd Herb Ellis song running through my mind getting lost in the maze back and forth, right to left, up and down, Jesus Christ Man, asked a guy in one of those purple jumpsuits pushing a mop, oh yes, he said, and pointed me in a certain direction, wow, I thought, can't they come up with better places to die?

Reached the 6th floor few patients in hallway one guy old and eyes red as fire, really old man, definitely was not long for the world and he moaned in constant pain and he cried and he shouted and the nurses just went about their business and the doctors were nowhere to be found and the other patients simply found him a nuisance, I walked by and saw that his slipper was off and I bent down and put it on him, he came as close to a smile as he was ever going to get again, I didn't know what to do so I moved past him into a room feeling down and out – my co-worker was there, name of Glen, big beard streaked with grey, seemingly short slicked-back hair but from behind you saw the long braid that went down to his ass, drove a Harley and had two trucks, he was laying on his side and there was a nurse sticking something up his ass, *for fuck's sake,* I said, and moved back out of the room...

Waited till she came out and asked if it was okay to see him, sure she said as unconcerned as a monkey scratching her tits on a Sunday afternoon in the hairy African mountains sky pregnant with dangers and the easy death-dance just a kiss away but he was sitting up and looking out a window – *hey my man, I said, how goes it?* – I could hear the sound of a jazz saxophone blowing from someone's radio down the hall, hmmmm, could be Coltrane I thought, or maybe Parker – *I'm alright,* he said, smiling weakly, *I'm alright –*

"But what the hell is wrong anyway, have they been able to tell you anything?"

"They haven't told me shit – I keep shitting and pissing blood, sometimes in chunks – stomach cancer most likely…"

He held in a sob –

"Hey buddy, it'll be okay, let's not fret till we know something, ok?"

"…yeah, sure….what's going on at work anyway?"

'Same old shit, Jim is an asshole, Billy is a delusional prick, our boss continues doing his imitation of Colonel Blake from MASH, you know, that's about it…"

"I don't know how that fucking place has lasted so long…I hate those guys…"

They hate you too, I thought…

"But the one thing the boss did right was hiring you…" He said –

Man oh man, I thought –


Didn't sleep much later that day kept thinking about Glen poor fucker didn't look good wasn't sure if he was going to make it eyes kinda glossed over or something, that sad and dreary glaze that comes to people when they are just about done with this asshole world but I sipped on a decaf coffee cuz I had developed an allergy to caffeine in recent years and "getting older" can kiss my ass never believe those idiots who tell ya that it's cool cuz it's a goddamn train wreck, and I was just at the beginning, looooooooooooong time to go, so the coffee went down well and sweet but my mind could not stop runnin' television on all droopy-eyed and strange things had to be a certain way man, don't you see? Don't you see the long-lost sadness waiting for you? Don't you see the cool runnin' graveyard extending a hand? Don't you see the morning-after jukebox all silent and scared? Life felt so cold at times that you just wonder what the whole damn thing is worth anyway, but I made my way downstairs and thought some music might calm the late-afternoon jangles put a record on the turntable, heard the needle scratch and the music kicked into the room, *"Echo and the bunnymen"*, CROCODILES, sat back and paused, moved forward and broke one of my rules, NEVER DRINK ON A WORKDAY - one won't hurt, I thought, just one –

Twenty minutes later I was on my fourth Rye and 7 and the music was blaring and I had smoked a joint and I felt like smiling – I was listening to The Velvet Underground but had a sudden urge for some Zeppelin so I slapped on the digital music and out came their second album and those hard rocking blues ripped apart the room and I poured two or three more drinks and another puff of smoke blew upwards towards the ceiling and suddenly my world felt almost complete, early afternoon man and I kept thinking about my job, kept thinking about stopping the drink - *listen buddy, you stop now, you can take a nap and still make the midnight shift* - and I thought of those knuckle-dragging morons I worked with and walking those long dark museum hallways with buffalos and polar bears and dinosaurs and ancient Natives all reaching out to me, this is frightening ol' boy, the music was now on random which was a cool thing about digital tunes but something with that sound ain't right man, it sounds too good, know what I mean jack? Me with my Rye listening to the blues and singing "oh mama, mama, mama, shake my thing", and everybody's in trouble in blues songs and the world don't give a shit, yeah, oh yeah, uh-huh – but what happens anyway? What happens when you die? What happens when the music's over? I had watched all those debates between the intellectual atheists and the pious theists, and Sam Harris telling the priests that they are delusional, and the priests telling Richard Dawkins that he's an evil shit and just doesn't get it, and Chris Hitchens (RIP ol' boy) with his intellectual diatribes tearing apart all that is magic, and man can't you see the egos spilling out into the room and running everything? Can't you see that no one is saying what they really feel, they just want to be *seen* in a certain way - the atheists begging to be viewed as intelligent, it's in the way they stand there and speak all that shit that only the formally educated speak and that the rest of us know means nothing, and the religious want to be seen as "good", as decent, as "faithful", as morally superior, *my unshakable faith, my lord, do you see it?*

No one tells the truth, even when they think they are, not a single one of us –

*I better fucking phone off work*, I said out loud, dialed the number and started pretending I was sick, the security guard on phone giving me a hard time, but seeing that people call off every second day at this place and I hadn't in years, I stopped pretending and just said, *Book me off, Jack, I ain't coming to work tonight* and cranked the music while he was still on the line then hung up and went straight for the Rye...

......................................

Hangover in hand I sat at the side of the bed –

"…feeling a bit better today…" He said, but he looked worse…

"Yeah, Glen, you look better…what they feeding you?"

"Look man…I don't know why everyone hates me at the job…I used to bring pizza in for everyone, I used give people rides home in winter…went way out of my way too, they didn't live close…I don't understand…"

"….forget it man, you don't want to listen to those assholes, fuck'em…"

"So, did you hear that latest Pink Floyd record?"

"That reunion thing?"

"Yeah, I think it was all instruments, no singing…."

"I heard a few tracks here and there…don't like it…"

"Man, I used to love that band, did so much drugs to that shit…"

'Didn't we all…"

"Dark Side Of The Moon, how good was that? That cash register at the beginning of 'Money'…"

"…how 'bout Wish You Were Here?"

"All that stuff from the 70's was fucking wild….Led Zeppelin 1…"

"Or 2, or 3, or 4…."

"Why do you think punk rockers bashed Zeppelin so much?"

"They were partly right, and partly wrong…y'know, at its best, punk is great, but so much of it is so fucking shitty, you wonder where the hell they get off talking about anything…"

"I hate that fucking place…"

"That place?"

"That place we work at…"

"Listen, you cause a lot of the shit there, Glen, you know that, right?"

A cleaner came in, young Philippine lady, broom in hand wearing headphones and Glen started in on her, she shouldn't be listening to music while working, she should clean the toilet better because there's a terrible stink coming from there, *get right in there*, he says, *get your face right in there*, and she went red looking like the tears were going to come down then walked out of the room – I glared at him –

"An asshole right to the end, hey Glen?"

He looked at me saying nothing but no sign that he did anything wrong, no sign that he regretted treating that young lady like shit, he was so wrapped up into himself and the world was so completely there for him that the possibility of being wrong never entered his head, even here at the end – *I'm 5 years old and I want what I want right now* – a single child no doubt who must have been spoiled rotten by his parents and had severe mommy issues, but I had enough for the day and my hangover was telling me to take off,

"I'll see you tomorrow man, I gotta go"

"Wait man, listen…"

I took off his voice trailing behind me…


Went to work that night and slowly cruised the hallways of the museum night-lights on and the shadows loomed large and splashed their images all over the walls and I turned corners and heard the usual noises and saw the usual sights but it never failed to take my breath away, it never failed to soothe my aching psyche, especially when I entered a certain diorama which was concerning a large ketch boat from 1668 called The Nonesuch about 160 feet in length with 200 hundred foot masts and it was recreated to the centimeter and it sat at a sea-port in old London which was also recreated in great detail with wooden rails and floor planks and buildings and it curved its way around the gigantic room dotted with barrels and cannons and stairwells that brought you to upper floors where you could look out into the sea and the sailors waiting for high tide, and it had its own bar called the 'Blind Pig' and you could sit in it at an ornate wooden table with clay mugs in front of you and a bartender pouring drinks long black mustache leather vest and pirate-looking patrons gloom all around and I said to myself then and there, *if and when I quit this job I am going to sneak in some booze on my last night and git drunk right here with these old boys,* I sat there for a few hours which was the cool thing about this job, being alone for 7 and ½ of the 8 hour shift, my own boss, do what I do, do it when I please, and they paid me decently for it as well first job of my life that did that, was used to treading water with minimum wage while I wrote on the side, all my life, every single job I had, barely paying the rent, sometimes not paying it at all and skipping out at midnight leaving every bit of furniture behind with just the clothes on my back looking for my next gig, the next kick at the can, the next big failure, but anyway I sat there – this section of the museum was left brightly lit 24/7 sounds of the ocean washing up on the shore and the seagulls singing sad and long and I closed my eyes and I thought of my wife and my daughter and my mother and my brother all feeling far away and low and I thought of my father, old man getting older, and my writing getting older too, and my tattered jeans with greasy black t-shirt in my dresser, and my guitar sitting in a corner screaming for attention, and my adventures living broke and wild and somewhere else man, all the people in my life full of meaning and hope and liking my crazy ways, I thought of God as well, I thought of him pulling wires behind a curtain of glass telling everyone, *"it's okay, people, stop panicking and being fools, it's all just a joke man, start loving things"*, and you gotta dig being alive cuz soon you will be dead, and maybe being dead is something grand and bright and beautiful but I ain't holding my breath, I thought about all of this and a whole lot more…and then, for the last time, I thought of Glen…

# SNAKE GUN HOWL

They sat across from each other. Man and woman. Large windows let in the sun from somewhere in the distance and the shadows stretched out across the floor. There was a bottle of something on the table between them and they both partook heavily.

"But…" She said,

"I know…" He said –

Sadness between them, they continued drinking and staring. There was once a child. But he was gone now. There were once friends, family, a life. That was gone too. Yet what was left was so damn hard to let go of, and nothing had been decided.

"You know, I tried, honey, I really did…" He said,

"No one is saying that you didn't…"

"I'm telling you, I couldn't have tried harder…"

"Whatever…what are we going to do, what the fuck?"

She remembered when they first met – how handsome he was, how charming, how decent and wild at the same time, how much they loved each other. She learned from him, it was immeasurable how much she learned. Books, films, and especially music, he taught her music above all. And in turn she taught him about sex.

"I still love…" He said,

"Don't…" She interrupted, "Please don't…."

"How about some music, do you want to listen to some music?"

She shrugged her shoulders but he thought he detected a faint smile. He put on *The Del Fuegos*, their first album. The music entered the room and with it came a sliver of sunshine.

"I remember…" She said, and she smiled and it was genuine and it was pure.

He smiled as well and for a second she looked 20 years old again and the music swelled around her and the sun outside the window seemed to grow large and proud and the shadows receded. She got up and danced. She danced until the end of the first song and then until the end of the second…then she sat down and started to cry. He just sat there and drank slowly and the tears almost came for him as well.

After a while, she dried her eyes. The tears stopped as suddenly as they began. She thought of a certain day walking the downtown streets. He had just published a novel and it looked like he could finally quit his day job. She had been so happy for him. She had been happier for him than she had ever been for herself. The clouds filled the sky and the rain just hung there taking its sweet time. It was beautiful. They held hands and their bodies touched and they walked the streets like they were teenagers in love.

Time went by and the book sold horribly and he never did quit his day job. Maybe that's what had done it for her. But how was that his fault? What type of horrible person was she to judge him for that? She knew he was a great writer, she knew it right down to her bones. It was the world that sucked, of that she was certain.

"I love your writing…" She said, "I…"

"I know….I know….are you hungry?"

"No…I hate food…I hate eating, that pause in things…that normalcy…."

"I know what you mean…I do…"

"Do we still have that *Replacements* album?"

"Which one?"

"That one I used to like so much…remember?"

"Was it *Pleased To Meet Me*?"

"Yeah, that's it…"

"Not on record…I think…on digital…"

"Don't you hate that digital shit?"

"You know I do…."

A brief moment flashed in his mind – laying in the tall grass…both of them almost naked…her blonde hair sparkling in the sun…her warm lips…her perfume in the air…

She got up and put the digital music on - *Pleased To Meet Me* – what sounds, what memories…all of it of yesterday, a yesterday better than today. She poured a drink then noticed his glass was empty. She filled it with ice and poured the brown liquid into it.

Three quarters full, just how he liked it. They had always liked drinking and it had never gotten ugly. They were lucky. It had destroyed some good friends of theirs. But for them, it was just something they liked doing - like eating a donut, like walking in the rain, like having sex.

"I didn't mean to do it…you know that, right?" He said,

"No…I don't know…."

"But…"

"I don't want to talk about it…"

"Remember when we went to Italy?"

"Yeah…" She smiled,

"When we hopped that train in Torino and took it out of town?"

"We just got off whenever we felt like it, all those small villages we saw…"

"We didn't even know where the hell we were…man…."

"What a beautiful country….it's so different from here…everything here is hard and ugly….commerce, money, work….I think we might have been happy there…"

"We were happy here…or have you forgotten?"

"Money, money, money…aren't you sick of how much people think about money? This is the richest country in the world and it's not enough…always more, more cars, more houses, more toys, bullshit piled on bullshit…."

"I know…I'm sick of everything money can buy, every bit of it…"

"But they trap you…and there's no getting away…"

"Maybe, you know, we can try…"

"Better people than us have tried…"

She lit a cigarette. The bracelets on her right wrist jingled. She had quit a few years earlier. She inhaled deeply and blew out large puffs that gathered around the table. He thought of joining her then thought against it. The digital music continued switching from Jazz to Blues to Rock and Roll then back again. He thought about growing up in the 70's, all that groove, all that easiness and wild sunshine. Or was he just romanticizing? Everyone thinks yesterday was better, right? Maybe one day this moment would be a great memory. But the music - he wasn't wrong there, no way man, the music back then was something else. She felt the same, even though she was younger. The modern age with its digital toys and smart phones and pop star mentality did not work for her. This ugliness contributed to the current state of their relationship, she was sure of this.

The kitchen counter was old and worn – the rest of the house felt the same. It was now 1 in the morning and it was a hot night. The booze didn't help. She crossed her legs and kicked her ankles. Her black pumps were off under the table. Her toes were painted deep red. Thick blonde hair was pinned up but the occasional curl hung loose and wild. She stared down at the floor. Her bronze skin glistened in the heat. A single bead of sweat trickled down her thigh losing itself somewhere around the calf. He stole glances at her and quickly turned away looking at the open door leading into the night. A dog barked. A siren far in the distance. A male voice screamed something violent. He undid the first two buttons on his shirt. The sweat gathered on his forehead.

"I was on welfare once…" He said,

"You never told me that…"

"It was a long time ago…I was really young, maybe 22…"

"How did you end up on welfare?"

"Oh, I don't remember – I probably just wanted to fuck around, you know…any young person can get a job…"

'What made you think about that?"

"I was just remembering how happy I was…for some damn reason, I was happy…"

Bubbles of moisture collected on her legs. She was beautiful, worn-out, but still beautiful. Their eyes met. He turned away. She gently put a hand on his shoulder. Her bracelets sang like chimes. With long slender fingers on his chin she turned his face.

"I know you didn't mean to do it…" She cried softly, then stopped, "I know…"

"Thank you…"

"It's not your fault…all of this…it's not your fault…"

Her bronze face was soaked in tears and sweat and her mascara was running. She wore a smile either on the verge of laughter or on the verge of deep sadness. The music had switched to Blues, something from Bukka White. It oozed into the room. The sounds of the neighborhood mingled with it. For a moment everything seemed to be in perfect rhythm. Then the music stopped and it was done.

He lit a cigarette and passed it to her then lit one for himself. He leaned back against the wall. She looked at the dog dish in the far corner. Then at the window over the sink. An oak tree sat outside making shadows. The tree branches stretched forwards looking like long, crackling fingers in the night. She felt it happen at that very moment.

"I remember…" She said.

# PETE'S STORE

When I was a kid in the 70's the corner stores were everywhere – small crowded brick shacks full of chocolate-bars milk-cartons sliced bread, pickles, cookies, butter, coca cola, potato chips, ice cream, baloney sandwiches, black and red licorice, juju beans, pizza pops, small toy soldiers, cantaloupe, watermelon, rotten bananas, rock and roll magazines and the comic books had their own rotating shelf right by the cash register...spin the rack around watch all those colors like a vibrato staccato of multi-limitations, see what the hell Spiderman was up to, see if he's still fucking around with that red-headed groovy chick that hung out with him after school...

Stores run by husband and wife of all races, small things really 'bout the size of a large working class basement with short aisles and product all stuffed together, I lived in little Italy a section of larger neighborhood called Fort Rouge and my neighborhood alone had 3 different stores each on corner of this-street and that-street, but the one we kids hung out at was Pete's Place on Arbuthnot and Fleet, Big Pete was Italian immigrated like me from old country and had wife no kids and a big black bastard of a German Shepherd in his back yard, real vicious prick....I was 10 years old friends Barney and Gordon and Mervin and Abe and Cindy and Lori and Marie, and my cousin Max, well we were always on that corner, always causing shit and laughing and running wild and cool and we were good kids, nothing crazy or violent, not us, the crazy and violent all around though, the crazy and violent was there aplenty,

"Hey Max" said Lori, "Look at Big Pete, he's pretending to read that magazine but he's eyeballing us…"

"What a goofball" Said Max, "Let's see if he comes over…HEY PETE, CAN YOU HELP ME FIND SOMETHING?"

"What? What do ya want?" Said Big Pete unmoving –

"Well, can you come here and help us?"

"Uggghh, what the hell you looking for?"

"WE, AHHH, WE ARE LOOKING FOR THE LATEST "MOON-KNIGHT" ISSUE…YOU GOT IT?"

"THE COMICS ARE ALL RIGHT HERE, FIND IT YOURSELVES…AND IF I SEE YOU GUYS HANGING AROUND THE OUTSIDE OF MY STORE, I'M GOING TO KICK YOUR ASS, GOT IT?"

Gordon threw a sack of flour in the air and it hit the ground and exploded, "whoooooooooooooooooooooo!" Pete goes nuts, "JESUS CHRIST, FUCKING KIDS, YOU'RE ALL DEAD….." Off we went with him on our ass flying down the street and through the schoolyard, off we went all jazzed and crazy and pure and the green/purple grass was everywhere and the large elm trees giving us cool shade in the hot summers and the wind at our heels our laughter echoing through little Italy rough and tough Italians hanging out windows of small two-story houses all bunched together tiny rectangle front yards, our school sat in the middle of the neighborhood giant building five or 6 floors made out of red brick my house right across the street could see the school at night in the darkness few windows lit up thought it looked like Dracula's castle giving me those cool beautiful nightmares waking up alive and refreshed and ready again and again...

*Gordon grew up and became a member of the local biker gang ending up in jail 10 years for armed robbery –*

Cruising those streets all day and night I was just a kid of 10 you know but back then the kids roamed free and loose and the neighborhood was full of people, old men playing Bocce in the schoolyard or cards at the many Italian cafes, housewives talking on corners laughing and complaining, young hippies smoking grass sitting with their backs against trees, drug dealers up and down the avenue in their corvettes and Camaros and their blow-dried Saturday-Night-Fever haircuts, but Barney was my best friend – met him one day after school walking through the schoolyard he was carrying a drawing and I asked him what it was, he showed me and I could see the Lone Ranger and Tonto shooting it out with villains of some kind or another and the Lone Ranger hid behind a rock and his bullets went up arching into a rainbow and came down on the villains also hiding behind a rock, WOW, I said, that is cool, and that started it....not just our legendary friendship spanning decades and many adventures but my love of art, writing and music – that drawing did it – I began to draw and draw and write and draw some more and we collected comic books and we made our own comics and then as a teenager I started playing guitar which eventually led to my writing and here we are - I owe all my creativity to Barney and The Lone Ranger and Tonto…

*Big Pete lived 'till 83 and died of an aneurism while visiting Catania, Sicily, the land of his birth –*

But one day all bored and restless and God giving us his juicy big grin with the sun always blinding bright and willing and us teasing the neighborhood girls with their jeans and sandals and ogling the older teenage versions in their jean shorts and bare feet walking on the cool grass in and out of the tree-lined streets, we decided to fuck with some older kids, old enough to drive these guys acted all tough and street-like but they weren't that tough, and we saw them sitting in one of the many small parks by the concrete wading pool which was never used and was full of broken beer bottles and empty cigarette packs and the teenagers were off to the right smoking grass, we began with the insults and the jibes and they would get up, and we would take off, and they would sit back down, then over again, and us laughing and laughing and Max strolling down the street right away joining in and Max just as close to me as anyone we 3 digging each other and our young lives like an early morning in the grass, just like that –

Max took it further and threw a banana peel in their direction but the wind took it and it just sort of landed in a flop a few feet from us – they laughed and gave us the finger called us fags, the whole bit, well, Max, having that beautiful Italian temper that he had, picked up the banana, walked slowly and calmly towards their cars and slammed the banana, and the slurpee he was drinking, right into one of their windshields, the whole scene exploded, they were after us!

We managed to give them a good run but our 10 year old legs were no match and they had us cornered against a tree slowly approaching, one of them pushed Barney to the ground, "fuck you!" said Max, the other two guys grabbed both of us and just then we heard it – "HEY FUCKERS, LEAVE THEM ALONE" There was my big brother with the family German Shepard on a thick leather leash chomping at the bit sun at Bro's back his figure all dark and shadow long thick hair blowing in the wind beside him a yellow Corvette and a short stocky fellow with thick curly hair leaning up against the open door, Frank Castelli, and we all knew what Frank Castelli did and we all knew what my older brother did….the situation ended right there and the boys dispersed and off went the Corvette with my brother and that crazy-ass German Shepard fading into the green of the neighborhood dusk coming fast…

*Frank Castelli later joined the local faction of the Italian Mob – 20 years later he was found dead in his car on the highway just approaching Montreal – he had been tortured and burned alive – word was he had turned snitch –*

Barney was a Native kid born in Camperville, Manitoba, came to the big city at age of 7 just before meeting me in that glorious schoolyard of yesteryear very tall lanky and funny as hell two sisters older brother parents cool easy people lived on same street as me just a block down on holy and funky Garwood Avenue, Max living on other side of neighborhood street called Mcmillan just a

10-15 walk from us but we had to cross busy street of Corydon where all the Italian cafes and bars and pool halls and city lights shone bright and deadly, so this was an adventure for us kids but the world and society were lenient back then and our parents didn't mind, or didn't care, either way just fine with me man anything but the shitty discourse of today-parenting and today-no-risk society, summer days and nights school out all us kids just hanging out at the park day and night till the sun went down and the racial tension in neighborhood cutting through the sweaty nights cuz little Italy in my corner of world wasn't like in the movies with just the Italians roaming and ruling the streets hanging out against brick walls and storefronts, no, our Piccola Italia was a multi-cultural place with many peoples from all over the world, the Italians were the main bunch, NOT the only bunch...

*Barney ended up being the lead singer in my bar-band and my songwriting partner – after 6 years of playing local bars and town halls he joined Greenpeace and sailed the world for 12 years – he remains my friend and in my life –*

One night us walking Max, Barney, Gordon, Cindy, Lori and myself the breeze spinning round the trees and the leaves rustling and the Camaros burning rubber car exhaust filling the neighborhood and the gasoline memories strolling down Mulvey Street we reached a corner where a young Pakistani man stood one hand in pocket other at his side cigarette in his teeth, well, he took a full-force swing at Gordon busting his nose and sending him sprawling to the ground then bolting down the back alley all of us shouting in fear and panic hell only 10 years old but Max took off after that prick myself stopping him and off we ran to my house where mother and father cleaned Gordon up then the old man takes us out in his car roaming the neighborhood looking for this freak, old man being tough as nails southern Italian short-stocky guy always ready to fuck someone up, but the guy seemed to disappear and the night ended....until.... word got to my older brother and, in turn, to Frank Castelli...a week later Pakistani fella found unconscious with two broken ribs and his teeth on the bloody sidewalk...

*Max got an education ending up with an office job and marrying a beautiful young Italian woman. They remain close to me and fully in my life.*

Somewhere in the middle of all that we would hear the 'adult' rumors, all the shit the grown-ups were up to, we'd hear it in the schoolyard and in the streets and under the trees, and Sam's old man was fucking the Calabrese broad from the bakery on Corydon, and Linda's mom was on pills and drank Jack Daniels in the afternoon, and Oliver's uncle worked for Murder Incorporated, and Albert from the pool hall on Mulvey Street owed money to mobsters from New York, and the East Indian fellow on Dudley Avenue was doing it with Big Pete's wife and Big Pete cruised for young chicks down the Corydon strip on Saturday nights, all true, all lies, all very, very real, us kids and the tall trees and the young gangsters and those beautiful street-corner-stores melting into a bar-room dream hazy and lazy just like an early morning in the grass, I tell ya, just like that....

# GASOLINE MEMORIES

- In the 20's we had Louis Armstrong, Bessie Smith, Sidney Bechet, Hemingway, Fitzgerald and Speakeasys – what we got today? –

-Video games, he said, as they sadly tuned their guitars –

-----------------------------------

- I've never met anyone that drinks like you, she said –

- How do you mean? – I said,

- You never turn into an asshole, she said –

-------------------------------------------

- When my dad died, he said –

- Yes? She said,

- Never mind, he said, got anything to eat?

- Ain't got shit, she said, as the moon disappears behind dark clouds –

-------------------------------------------

- I like when the saxophone solos at the end, he said –

- I only like punk rock, he replied –

- What about film noir? He said –

- Talk fucking English, I'm Canadian, he said –

-------------------------------------------

A cigarette was lit and the room went black -

- That way they do it, he said –

- Do what? She said –

- The way *they* make you work for them – the way they trick you with money – he said –

- Well what else do you want? She said -

- The night isn't long enough, darlin', he said, and they rolled over and fucked again –

-------------------------------------------------------------

- Didn't your Poppa ever teach you how to treat a girl? She said
–

- No, but he kicked my ass day and night, he said –

- Did you deserve it? She said –

- Sure did, he said, and the silence screamed and the devils
roared –


And I'm walking through the devil infested streets, and all I see
are lights greasy and wanting, and all I see is violence and blood-
red intentions, and all I see are the generals feasting on flesh, and
there was an old friend of mine standing at a street corner with
back against telephone pole just watching the cars go by and the
lights from the liquor store red and blue and purple and orange
and yellow and it's metal-to-metal striking that note just right and
the midnight crazies looking to fuck someone up, but we stop and
talk and we're not afraid and we're not unhappy and we're even
bored kinda feeling the end of something,

"I'm just bored with all of this" I say,

He nods and smiles sadly and I wave goodbye and I see all the
street-junkies hobbling along with their toothless grins and their
one-note thinking, and I see the young girls with sad smiles holding
on to nothing at all the predators never far, and I think of losing
*her* suddenly and that tragic afternoon under the sun, sometimes a
nice car pulls up to the liquor store and the well-groomed move

forward their intentions and true meaning as rotten as everybody else's and the bank accounts ring like a bell as their fucked-up night-world is about to begin, I think of the 1920's and Dixieland jazz and Billy Holiday and sipping on cold gin at a Parisian café while Picasso strolls by screaming something wild and crazy, and the young victims died in back alleys then as they do now and as long as people are involved, the shit flows, and I need all your love, baby, all of it day and night…

But I see something else now, I see a movie theater with light bulbs shining on the edge of the billboard full of smiling ideas, and I see a late-night pizza joint with small line-up of guys and gals laughing into the darkness, and I see a middle-aged couple kissing in front of a closed record store and I think of good friends and screaming good times and I'm talking about the light-filled moments everywhere all around –

- and it's day-time now and I am by a river beams of golden light coming through trees and green all around wooded path leading me into that cool-sunshine shiver and I don't hesitate, I don't hesitate to smile and to laugh and to feel alright, and the river ripples in the wind bright-diamond-flickers on its surface, opposite bank showing a few apartment buildings sprouting out from the ever-present green of the ever-present trees, a young woman jogs by thighs jiggling in the hot morning shadow, old man walks slowly leaning on cane smiling lovely and new his youth bubbling just under the surface, and we all wanna get along don't we, between closed teeth she swears again, between lips parted he smokes and says goodbye, and the college students continue with their misguided learnings, and the proletarians can all kiss my ass, and the rejected rejects triumph once again, and above the skyscrapers the superheroes continue their homo-erotic wrestling, I shake god's hand and give him a wink, he winks back and smiles and scratches his ass, all my love to you I say, and mine to you he says, then he cranks the electric guitar and starts playing some rock and roll, and all across the universe and beyond and through the back-alley love affairs and the switchblade mornings,

the inside of my mind screams happy thoughts -

# CLAUDIA

It wasn't pornography –

There were people, men and women, who liked getting sat on and stood on and wrestled down to the carpet and the internet was loaded with it and there was money to be made and seeing she had a hard time doing anything else, she started….it was all amateur stuff, just herself, some pot, some willing dude or dudette, and a camera…and a bikini, maybe some sexy underwear, no nudity, no sex at all, nothing like that, and man, she made some serious money lived in high-rise downtown with floor-to-ceiling windows shag carpet like walking on clouds and she wrote poetry at night and even tried her hand at a screenplay and just tried dealing with all this shit and the no-denying-guilt that crept up on her from time to time…

Her name was Claudia –

She set the camera in a corner of the room, adjusted it for proper framing, then took a sip of her whiskey -

"Hmmmm, you might have to move a bit to your left" She said,

"Like this?" said the young lady laying on the carpet –

"Yeah, just like that" said Claudia,

The young lady laid there in a purple bikini and breathed in nervously – she was 5 feet tall, 95 pounds, blonde hair – Claudia was 5'10", 175 pounds, flat stomach, small waist, all the weight in the thighs and ass…

She put *Dire Straits* on, the first album, it was the only one she liked from the band, then she lit a joint inhaling deeply – pooooooooooooooof, shhhhhhhhhhhh….

"You want some?" said Claudia –

"No…well, maybe…"

"Okay, here then…"

The small woman started getting up –

"Oh no" Said Claudia, "Stay right there…"

She walked over and placed the joint in the lips of the girl on the carpet and the girl inhaled nervously, Claudia smiled, the girl inhaled again…then Claudia stuck the joint in an ashtray, lit a cigarette, and stood on the girl with both feet on her chest long dark hair wild and loose her red underwear shining in the gloom…the girl let out a deep breath and the veins on her neck bulged…it continued from there –


After taking a shower she uploaded the clip to her webpage in wet hair and bathrobe, set the price, and sat back – the orders came in almost immediately and she smiled and drank wine and began writing checking on her sales sporadically, writing and dreaming of being a full-time poet maybe a screenwriter famous or near-famous but doing just that one thing for a living, just that one thing…she loved getting almost-drunk and writing and playing at being something else, a thousand miles from today, she said to herself…her writing desk was right by the floor-to-ceiling windows and as she put the words down on the page the city lights shone bright into the dark room and the skyscrapers towered over and around her and the street-level jive-talk jabbed and lunged and smoked crimson cigarettes like an Orphan-Annie-Opera or a Ray Manzarek keyboard solo and she liked being alone for some of the time, and with people for some of the time…around 3 in the morning and 8 or 9 pages later she hit the sack feeling good and alive and drunk-happy –

---------------------------------------------------------

---

"Claudia – Claudia, what the fuck?"

"Yeah, yeah, fuck, I'm here, I'm here!" Said Claudia –

They were at an outdoor café on a trendy street sun beating down heavy and lost Claudia's sister staring at her across table couple of Vodka Oranges in front of them full ashtray young waiter circling room,

"Christ, Claudia, you fucking disappear lately, what the hell's bugging you?" Said the sister –

"Nothing, Annie, nothing at all – just a lot of work, you know…what's happening, baby?"

"Everything's cool, everything's cool…"

"Those boys are so beautiful, Annie, you are so lucky"

"Yeah, they are….in a few years Tony will be a teenager, for fuck's sake, we're getting old…" She took a drag and a drink,

"Speak for yourself, girl…"

"You're not too far away, little sis, stop acting like (drunken pause) like you're a young party chick…"

They both laughed and drank and dug each other –

"How about you, girl, anyone hanging around? Anyone speciallllllllllllllll…"

"No one…that I know of" She thought of all her online admirers,

"Ah, fuck it, it's overrated anyway…who needs some idiot hanging around all the time?"

They both laughed and hit glasses –

"Everything's okay with you and John, right?" Said Claudia,

"Yeah, yeah, men are fucking morons, you know?"

"I hear ya…"

"Don't you think that sometimes we would be better off single? Just get fucked whenever we feel like it, make them give us children, then fuck the hell off!"

"Ha, ha, ha….when are they going to learn how to fuck a woman anyway, I mean a good, proper fuck?"

"They will never learn…I swear, I deserve an Oscar the way I act with John"

They laugh again –

"Hey, Claudia, if you ever get tired of that secretary job, our offer still stands, you know?"

"Me work in a restaurant? That's funny"

"Just sayin', ya dig?"

Just tell her, thought Claudia to herself, just tell her…

"Nah, I dig my job…really dig it…"

-------------------------------------------------------------------------------

She couldn't bring herself to tell anyone what she really did even though she knew there was nothing wrong with it, but she also knew that most people suck and can't see beyond the tip of their nose, this is what she thought on a park bench watching the river shine and roll in front of her and the ducks moved slowly with their asses in the air and the wind was light sun up high and warm, some people jogged down the river-walkway, some people strolled, some people just sat there getting high, Claudia felt strong and happy and she could feel the electricity surging through her body in shocks and waves of purple rain, and she was driving on 9 like a shadow past a motel and the elm trees lined up like prizes in the pretty sunshine - I miss you, she said to herself getting suddenly sad, I really miss you - but sadness disappears quickly on days like these as couple of kids race by on their bikes and she playfully sticks her tongue out and they return the favor, ok, she said to herself, smile you crazy bitch, and she got up and walked away in her jean shorts and flip-flops her olive-skin-thighs moving from side to side and the feeling in the air like glass, like surging delight, like lazy Vodka Orange Sundays…


She sat on a chair at a downtown café across from her brother, her younger brother, smoking cigarettes and drinking White Russians and they even snuck around the corner and smoked a joint –

"So, Mark, you still fucking that young chick?" Said Claudia,

He burst out laughing, "What the fuck, what young chick?"

"That German girl, that exchange student?"

"Among others…"

"You're a dog!"

"Rabid…buy me another drink, will ya?"

"Sure thing, I got nothing but money and time…"

Drinks came, they both flirted with the waitress, then they continued –

"You make a lot of money for a secretary, sure you're not selling grass on the side or something?"

"Well, my little pukey brother, there's always something on the side, ya dig?"

"Yeah, I dig, I dig…I always figured you were sexually adventurous, maybe a closet bisexual… "

Between laughing fits, "You crazy fucker, ha ha ha ha, I like dick, don't worry…"

"Oh, I'm not worried, just sayin', I would still love you, ha ha ha ha…"

"So how's College, kid?"

"C'mon, man, do we have to get serious?"

"No, no, no, just wondering, you know? Gotta make sure my little bro is doing well, that's all…"

"I don't know, I just can't get into it, know what I mean? It's not that I haven't tried, I don't know…"

"Well, all you can do is try"

"I just want to be happy, Claudia, that's all…"

"Yeah, for sure, I hear ya…just live your life, Mark…as you see it…"

Just tell him, she thought to herself, just tell him –

"Maybe I'll become a street-poet" Said Mark,

"Yeah, mom and dad will love that" Sarcastically,

The sadness kind of hovered around them and settled in the air – then they laughed about that thing they did when they were kids, or maybe it was that other thing when they were teenagers, or maybe it had nothing to do with them at all, but they laughed anyway and it started to rain the drops hitting the umbrella above their head making that cool sound and the sidewalk slick and groovy and full of something dangerous and they said goodbye on the corner hugging and letting the rain fall all over and around them and Mark clicked his heels and danced away singing the Bowie song Suffragette City loud and proud and Claudia smiled, laughed, then walked away sadly…

Few days later she became reacquainted with an ex-boyfriend, Gary Miles they called him, had long hair parted in the middle and a goofy grin and they went out and got drunk and saw alternative rock bands and cruised through the cool arty parts of town and hung out at poetry readings and blues jams and rock and roll parties and they had sex morning noon and night and he played guitar in a jazz band that was a local legend and she told him the same secretary lie she told everyone else, that she worked in an insurance office and her boss paid her generously and it was good, and she really dug him and wow, man, it was all coming alive for her…

But then…as it does…life decided to fuck with her…

What she did for a living was posted all over social media – her picture – her name - and it was derided – and it was judged – and it was condemned –

Annie was telling Claudia about it at a quiet downtown bar –

"Jesus Christ, Claudia, what the fuck?"

Claudia said nothing –

"This is your "secretary" job?"

The tears fell down Claudia's face –

"…who knows?" Said Claudia –

"It's all over fucking facebook, everybody fucking knows, Claudia!"

"Your kids?"

"YES, FUCK, YES!"

"Mom and dad?"

"THEY ARE FUCKING FREAKIN' OUT! Well what the fuck, Claudia? This is what you do for a living? It's sick…"

"…it…is…not sick…"

Waiter came around and Claudia ordered a double Gin and ice as she downed her third in the last 10 minutes…

'Well what the fuck is it, Claudia, is it normal? You like to sit on people, what the fuck, you get paid for it?"

Claudia's drink came…she took a long pull…her eyes were wet but the tears had stopped falling…

"…who…did this…?"

"Who fucking knows or cares? An ex-boyfriend maybe…someone you pissed off and dumped, God knows there are enough of them…"

"…that's enough, Annie…I'm sick of your moral superiority - I am not doing anything wrong…"

"It's fucking weird, okay, Claudia? It's humiliating!"

"What is fucking weird about it, huh? What is fucking weird about making someone feel good, about feeling good while doing it, what the fuck? There's nothing kinky going on in your bedroom, or in your head? Huh? Nothing?"

Annie liked to get tied up and spanked and fucked up the ass by her husband while being insulted in the worst ways imaginable – she could not have sex without this - yet she didn't give it a thought, she went shopping at the local food mart, she had chats with neighbors about their children, she went to parent/teacher meetings, she had breakfast and made lunch and watched sitcoms – she was even thinking of having an affair…

"Nothing, Annie? Jesus Christ, I'm not even having sex, fuck! Everyone has their clothes on - and even if they didn't - for fuck's sake, Annie, how is this any weirder than what "normal" people do in their bedrooms every fucking night?"

"How do I explain this to my kids, your fucking niece and nephews? How do you expect mom and dad to understand this?"

"Stick that moral judgement up your ass, Annie…" She downed her drink and stood up forcefully knocking her chair over "And you can tell Mom and Dad to go fuck themselves!"

She stormed off and Annie called out to her two or three times then called her a BITCH as Claudia turned the corner and started running going nowhere really fast and the clouds turned to night and she sat on a bench out of breath and far away, and nothing in her head could stop the screaming and the sounds of the street were jagged and violent and the night sounds far away and immediate and so fucking sad she lit a cigarette her hand trembling and her chest beating - she called Gary and he picked up after one ring – she could hear him breathing but nothing was said – she started to say something and Gary hung up and then just like a bell in the distance he was gone…she wandered around the downtown and a young man stood on a corner singing Verdi and an old man sat by a newspaper stand drinking Vodka and snapping his fingers to the music in his head and just across the street a man in his underwear went running by and a group of young kids followed on skateboards, Claudia reached a liquor store, went inside and bought a bottle of Rye, went back outside and sat right beside the old man snapping his fingers, the old fucker smiled and continued with whatever was happening inside his head and she sat there, and she cried, then she stopped, then she started drinking…

An hour later she walked up to her apartment past the doorman and a few glaring tenants and through the glass enclosed front lobby to the elevators all the way up to the 31$^{st}$ floor down the brightly lit hall her flip-flops squeaking in the silence and one of the neighbors watched her through his peephole as he did every night, "what a fucking beauty" he said to himself, "what a fucking beauty", she reached her door and went inside – she stripped naked then put on a pair of purple thongs and a tight bra of the same color…she sprayed a touch of perfume on her ass and pussy…on her phone there was a message from her parents – never to call them again – then one from her little brother – it just said "Claudia, what the fuck? Call me…." For a second she thought of that young guy she saw every day in the skywalks – did their eyes meet that one time - then she thought of the artist sitting in his coveralls at the end of the skyline and the flowerpot he was always painting and the way the sun entered the room and lit up the artwork – would he ever finish it, she thought – phone rang and Claudia let it go to the answering machine - Annie calling her a slut, whore, useless bitch and on it went – the anger in her rose like fire – the door to her apartment opened –

"Claudia, I've been knocking for a while…" It was the young 95 pound blonde, arrived for her session -

Claudia looked at her with unprecedented fury –

"Your door was unlocked…I…"

She ran at the blonde and grabbed her by the hair throwing her across the room with such force she bounced when she landed hitting the glass coffee-table and sending everything up in the air –

"Take that fucking raincoat off…" Claudia said gritting her teeth –

The blonde did revealing her red bikini underneath – Claudia stood over her then kneeled down and sat on her chest really hard as the blonde expelled air feeling the 80 pound difference – Claudia pinned the blonde's forearms with her knees and sat high up on her chest her crotch touching the blonde's chin – then she moved up and sat on her face with her pussy right on the blonde's mouth pressing down on her jaw – within minutes the blonde's eyes filled with tears – and it wasn't about to end anytime soon….

# CARLO AND GIANNI

On the way to Gassino – my uncle Gianni drove his Ferrari right through the city of Torino with me in tow 13 year old diggin' this fancy-flight to hell and we burst through the piazzas and the narrow streets and the downtown-running like a bolt of sweet lighting and to me and my youth-mind fire lit up the roads behind us and I looked at my uncle Gianni and dug what I saw, I saw an outlaw somewhere around 33 or 34 years old good-looking and wild slightly balding and just a shit-load of fun and you felt like something was happening around him, like something was *always* happening around him, and he reminded you of Roger Moore as The Saint, he had all the money and the cars and the cool apartments and continuous trips up and down Italy but no one knew how the hell he managed it going from shady business to business, job to job, thing to thing - but in Italy towns and cities are all close together so when you leave one you land in another immediately unlike Canada where you drive for miles through wild-country with those beautiful endless trees and all that green and brown and red and orange and yellow and man, before you see a town or a gas station or even a person the day turns to night, but there we were driving through San Mauro all a blur of happiness and thrill-seeking and my uncle looking sideways at me laughing lighting one cigarette after the other throwing them out the window after just a few puffs, we paused at a villa deep into the hill off the road with three or four separate apartments on the second level and Gianni tells me he has some business to conduct, "just wait in the car, kid, I'll be right back", and I saw a young woman in black negligee greet him at the front entrance and even as an adolescent I knew the score, I knew my uncle Gianni liked to fuck chicks, and he liked to fuck as many of them as possible, and I wondered if my aunt knew that, but the hell with it, I thought, they're the grown-ups, let them deal with this bullshit – and there came my Zio about half an hour later in his dress pants and dress shirt, expensive black shoes and 200 hundred dollar sunglasses, all piss and vinegar and triumph-grin as he gets in, lights a smoke, hands me 5000 liras (about 5 bucks), and off the Ferrari  went gravel shooting out from behind rubber and steel and non-conform-motherfucker ready to rumble baby, car takes a beautiful swerve as we enter Gassino and go up and up whole town built on the foothills of the Italian Alps in Northern Italy and the stone houses fly by in a blur, and young wives scream at each other from the balconies of two-storey apartment houses, and cafes and grocery stores and the sole movie theatre run behind us as the street keeps winding its way through the village to the steep gravel leading to my villa where he paused, shifted gears, and went roaring up the hill right to the end of the road – the car stopped, he beeped the horn, and then off went that monster-engine the silence suddenly deafening…

My aunt Graziella, his wife, stood at the entrance of our villa waiting in tight jeans, big smile, long red hair so young and beautiful and obviously in love – Gianni smiled back visibly excited and happy – they were in love, despite it all, they were in love…


Uncle Carlo was the exact opposite, loyal to his wife, steady work as a baker, family man with kids and a home and completely devoted to all of it…but he was every bit as cool as Gianni with a full head of thick brown hair parted on the side, looked and dressed like James Bond, the Roger Moore version, drove an Italian sport scar, a 124, really loaded piece of machinery all blue and metallic and sinew and it was streamlined like a shark and it was a convertible as we flew down Via Roma, Torino's main artery, and the expensive shops were there with the expensive people and the marble archways covered the street loaded with guys and gals looking for somewhere to spend their filthy money and all the outdoor patios full with the idle rich and the idle poor drinking espressos and cappuccinos and Grappa and Cinzani and Martinis and Gin-and-Tonics and Carlo smiled and kept lighting Marlboros in quick succession the wind tearing through our hair, and the Trams on their electric tracks making their way through the downtown and all those tiny cars racing down the street and double parking the noise level so excessive and drastic it went through me like a bolt of electric-orange, he took me to the soccer game where Torino was playing, took me to every single home game for the 3 years I lived there, and there we were in the stands, Pepper and Sausage sandwich in our hands our team coming out onto the field leisurely their red uniforms and bulging thigh muscles gleaming in the sun and the green field so damn beautiful and perfectly kept, my uncle chatting with everyone shaking hands and shouting and laughing and everyone loved Carlo and he loved them back and showed and got nothing but respect man – this was the last game of the year summer of 1977 and Torino was one point away from its rival, Juventus, also from the city of Torino, with the third team being behind 16 or 17 points - it had been a thrilling record breaking year with both teams being the clear runaways right from the start leaving the rest in the dust and in the realm of sweet-fuck-all - so there we were – last game – for Torino to win the championship they had to win and Juventus had to lose – if Juventus tied and Torino won, they would have to play the tie-breaker, one game, one only, winner take all, which Juventus did not want to happen as it lost both games to them during the season and it had been leaked that they were somewhat intimidated by Torino's aggressive Brazilian always-in-attack style of play, complete opposite to the Juventus defensive, counter-attack game….so everyone had eyes on the field and ears glued to small transistor radios trying to found out what the hell Juventus was doing, 60,000 people man, it was one monstrous and beautiful sound – Torino went up one goal – then a few minutes later, it went up two – championship or not, the team was, as usual, playing its fucking guts out and they were going to give us a show on this last day, half-time came up and still no news from Juventus but suddenly a nuclear wave of cheer went through the stadium and I heard one guy with radio in hand say, THEY'RE DOWN ONE, FUCKING JUVENTUS IS DOWN ONE!"

Uncle Carlo went crazy man, and the wine bottle was soon in his hands and the happiness in his face was something I will never forget, and I hugged him and felt really good like the world was going to be alright after all and my life nothing but triumphs and good times and laughter without end, and the teams came out for round two and Torino looked confident and in my young eyes like champions ready to hit the champagne and the late-night party-broads with fur coats covering naked bodies steamy and willing, in no time Torino went up 3-0, then the other team scored making it 3-1 but in soccer coming back from two goals down is almost impossible, and certainly not likely against a powerhouse team like this, but then it happened – word came down the pike Juventus was up 3-1 – the silence swept from section to section – I saw the team react, look up to the stands and realize that, perhaps, the dream was over – there were ten minutes left to play and everyone looked stunned – then somewhere in the distance someone shouted, FORZA TORO! That was the team cheer – it picked up slowly, then gained momentum, then I saw my uncle Carlo start screaming it at the top of his lungs and the coach on the field clapped his hands and encouraged the players and they started once again as the stadium exploded…

And Torino went on a tear slamming two more goals into them making the score 5 - 1 and just playing a beautiful attack mode soccer bringing the crowd to its feet time and time again – the news from Juventus was silent and the crowd waited and sang and hoped and got drunk, including Carlo, but in the end Juventus took the game 3 – 1 winning its 16th championship (a world record), and I turned towards my uncle and he had tears in his eyes and this moment I did not forget...


We had family dinners on Sundays after the game with Carlo and Gianni and my old man and mom and grandmothers and great-grandmothers and my cousins and my brother and the noise level in that small corner of the world was enough to wake the moon and to rouse all the street people on the planet into dank rebellion, Gianni telling his travel stories and Carlo talking about his times in Sicily and my old man telling us about riding his ten-speed across Italy and all of us happy and the times were bright and meaningful even with the usual miserable bullshit surrounding all families as Carlo and his family moved to Canada with us, Gianni staying behind – they both got divorced eventually, one in Canada, the other in Italy –

And now, 2016, their wives are dead...

My uncle Gianni had a stroke last year and is in a care facility in Rome unable to speak or walk but has recently made progress and can now eat on his own -

My uncle Carlo is remarried, 79 years old, and teaches baking at a college in Winnipeg and still has all his hair now gone grey and still looks like Roger Moore– he had a heart attack some years back but recovered fully and is planning his final trip to Italy to see his brother Gianni –

No more cruising down the Italian highways, no more soccer games on hot Sunday afternoons, the Ferrari is dead and gone but I am in love, and I am married, her name is Izzy, and we are working-class-broke in Winnipeg on this cold winter night the snow draping over the rooftops of the neighborhood and tonight she is making Pasta Bolognese as I write these words and the aromas of fresh tomatoes and basil fills the house and I suddenly remember this is one of Uncle Gianni's recipes, I even remember the day back in Gassino when he was showing my mom how to make it as I sat at the kitchen table, the sun outside shining through the kitchen windows, shining gently on my face...

# OPENING NIGHT

We had played many house parties in front of hundreds of people but this was our first professional gig, a bar-gig, an actual stage, lights, action, chicks, drugs, booze and rock and roll I was 19 years old living with parents but seed for urban inner-city shit already brewing inside and I had co-written all the songs with the singer who was my childhood friend, Barney, he was tall and wild and righteous baby long beautiful black hair aboriginal kid best friends since we were 7 years old and we were still riding high and full of piss and vinegar, bar was a seedy hotel on the South Side and we sat in the band room filthy place with broken down bed no sheets, stained mattress and small desk in corner but it had windows leading out to the roof which faced the river and all those green trees and the crime riddled street below with bums and street people throwing up last night's fun, we sat on the roof drinking beer and whiskey and smoking pot...well, Barney and I smoked pot, the bass player (Ronnie) and the drummer (high school friend named Nazzie) desisted thinking it would make them nervous but show was a few hours away so everyone was cool and easy with all the life-problems we had – Barney's parents were in the middle of divorce and it was nasty and painful and I saw it in his eyes, Nazzie's girlfriend had walked after cheating on him with a friend and his dad was an alcoholic, my relationship of 3 years was dwindling girlfriend and I drifting apart and feeling blue and my mother had just discovered a lump on her breast and she was waiting for results as I sat there looking at the sky feeling high and ready and doubtful and mighty and fearful all at the same time,

"How you feeling asshole?" Said Nazzie,

"Fine, motherfucker" I said,

"Pass me a beer"

Commotion from street below people arguing about something stupid, girl whooo-hoooing into the night, guy acting tough, other guy giving it back, GIMMEE THAT SHIT ASSHOLE! FUCK YOU, MOTHERFUCK!

"Hey, why you guys acting like assholes?" Said Barney, "You should be digging yourselves, one day you'll all be dead"

"WHO THE FUCK ARE YOU, ASSHOLE?"

"YEAH, PRICK, COME DOWN HERE, WE'LL KICK YOUR TEETH IN!"

"FUCK YOUR MOTHER!" I said,

"AND YOUR UNCLE, DICKWAD!" Said Ronnie,

And it went back and forth roof being only three stories up till bar bouncer walked outside and told those idiots to keep moving, which they did pretty damn fast bouncer large and ugly and looking real mean, so we lit cigarettes and the cars kept racing down the street we talked and laughed and argued but we got along well compared to all the other bands we had known always freaking out and fighting for power and being all masculine bullshit and unoriginal, no, we were good friends, we dug each other, and, if I may so myself, were a real good rock and roll band that could kick some serious ass – people started showing up, friends old and new and soon the room was full and it was a party and we were getting ready man, and it was like-wow-wipeout moving slow and easy through her bar-tight legs spread neon jungle bright smile deeply caressing all my problems away, young chick beside me was old high school friend we had fucked in hockey rink hot summer night few years back she all excited that we were finally on stage,

"You guys sound like a punk-blues band" She said, "Love the way you play that guitar"

Nazzie was moving around the room talking shit to all and sundry and we dug the Nazz, short guy with long curly hair and John Lennon glasses talking to Barney pissing him off somehow Barney moving from side to side back and forth smoking pot like a demon, Ronnie was a drinker youngest in group barely 18 classically trained played bass like John Entwistle later in life becoming a jazz teacher, well, he usually didn't talk much didn't do much but tonight all energy and bright lights, so I started thinking – I started thinking – everything tuned out and seemed to slow right down to nothing my stoned mind playing tricks – I started thinking about my mother, about the lump on her breast, about what might possibly happen, a sudden wave of heavy depression ran over me head to toe, I left the room went downstairs past hallways and stairwells dirty carpets cigarette burns old drunks forgotten landladies guy selling beer behind metal bars, other dude selling cigarettes behind counter long mustache listening to The Clash on small radio, I found a payphone and dialed a number –

My mom answered the phone – we spoke in Italian – I could tell she had been crying -

"…do you know anything yet?" I asked,

"…no, but don't you dare worry about this tonight, this is your night, Ziggy, don't worry about me…"

"How can I not?"

"C'mon, these things happen all the time, it's probably nothing, you know that, right? How are things anyway, are you nervous?"

"Not at all…just worried…about you…"

"Nothing to worry about, I'm telling you…how do you kids say? Rock and roll!"

Then she laughed – and the laugher made me feel better – and we spoke some more - and said goodbye – but then something happened, I turned around and through the entrance of the bar I saw something extraordinary – the fucking place was packed and people were running around, and the room was filled with smoke, and I could smell marijuana, and I could hear the swell of the crowd and the excitement hanging in the air…

Went back upstairs saw the boys trying to look all cool and easy and chuckled to myself – I tugged on Barney's sleeve as he tried to make a young chick,

"What, what, I'm kinda busy" He said,

"It's a packed house, man...."

"What?"

"Packed house..." I smiled,

"Jesus..."

He went and told Nazz and Ronnie – I saw their faces drop – I busted up the party and everyone headed for the bar except for the band –

"Wow..." Said Barney,

"...yeah..." Said Ronnie –

"What's wrong with you guys?" I said "Isn't this what we wanted?"

"Yeah, but I thought there would just be a few people tonight, maybe a few more tomorrow...you know...so I could slowly get used to it..."

"Me too..." Said Nazzie –

"Not me, baby" I said "I want as many people as possible to see us, right from the start man...we've played a shitload of house-parties, what's the difference here?"

"I don't know, the lights, the stage..."

"Fuck it, man, it's just people, they're here to watch US, remember, they are here for US...don't worry if we fuck up, it's rock and roll, just play it loose, ya dig?"

They nodded, smiled and nervously agreed –

"Besides" I said, "We fucking kick ass!"

"Alright, Ziggy, do we have that part in "Nickels and Dimes" down?" Said Nazzie,

I picked up my guitar and played the part, the chorus and bridge – Nazzie played the drums on the desk and it seemed like we had it down pat –

"Wait, Ziggy, that part where the solo kicks in, am I coming in on the first note? Or am I waiting a few hits?"

"It's right on the note, Ronnie" Said Barney "Play it, Ziggy…"

I did –

"See?" Said Barney, "The second he starts the lead, you come right in…"

Barney and me smoked a joint then we moved downstairs and went into the bar – the way it was set up you had to walk through the entire room to the stage guitars in hand and the crowd cheered the second they saw us all eager for some live music - I looked around there were a mix of old friends and strangers and biker-looking types and college fringe types, saw our manager behind the sound board, saw my dwindling girlfriend at a table with friends, saw my cousin Max and my brother and a few hot chicks at the front table in jean shorts and tank-tops –

The lights went down, I turned up the guitar, and we went right into it…

# A COUPLE OF DUDES

"Lookit that chick, whew, lookit that ass baby!"

"Don't act like a jackass, dude – but yeah, wow, what an ass!"

Then they saw that little guy with the Beatles' haircut get up and follow "the ass" down the skyway and they talked some more then moved forward on a mission – their mission being to purchase tickets for the show at The Rendevous Concert Hall that night featuring their favorite band, That Petrol Emotion – the only problem – they didn't have a penny between them...

"So how much are tickets?" Said Darryl as they walked the downtown streets,

"I think they're 14, 15 bucks, something like that?" Said Paul –

"Well what kind of fucking losers are we that we can't come up with 30 fucking dollars between the two of us?"

"Don't you worry, man, we'll find a way, we'll find a goddamn way!"

"Well you'd better find a street-corner somewhere and put your hat in hand, loser"

"Just follow my lead, jackass, we is going! Like Cleopatra into Rome, baby! Fuck, if Cleopatra in ancient Egypt could figure out how to fuck and not get pregnant, then we –

"- How the fuck did she do that?" Said Darryl,

"Using alligator shit, man"

They walked by a pawn shop and the high light black diamond stolen and ready glittered for a moment and then a cigarette was lit and blue smoke flew straight to the sky and then nothing was the same,

"She stuck alligator shit up her pussy?"

"Oh yeah, man, so she could just get fucked without problems, ya dig?"

"Well who was she fucking?"

"Everybody…she was the queen of the Nile, man"

"Where was her man, wasn't she married to that –

"Yeah, that fucker Antony…well you don't think that she was just sitting in her room reading fables as her man went away for months on end fighting this war and that and fucking with everyone's shit, do you?"

"Well no, but I didn't think that she was fucking every piss boy in the square, you know? I mean she was a queen, what the fuck? - Hey, how about your mom? Think she can help us out?"

"I am due for a visit…"

"She doing alright, man?"

"After the divorce, no one did alright…"

"I hear ya, man…okay, let's go, I need to get drunk and high and fucking see **THAT PETROL EMOTION!**"


And in the warm summer night they moved forward knowing nothing, doing nothing, and dear prudence was once their friend in the sunny sky falling but we don't give a shit, do we? Approaching Paul's mom in her inner-city one-story-shack warm and tired they are inside and sitting and talking and looking –

Paul's mom all gone and almost spent but not quite she gave them fried egg sandwiches  and some homemade beer and she drank too till she git what she git,

"OH Darryl, you are sooooo handsome, why I remember when you were just a little shit, 5 years old running these streets right here in front of the house, boy what darlings you both were…"

Then she took a long pull of her whiskey and a drag of her cigarette –

"You kids want cigarettes? Here, here, help yourselves, I get them from the U.S., a friend of mine goes there once a month – they're dirt cheap, help yourselves, my baby boy!"

She kissed her son and grabbed his cheeks –

"What long hair you both have, goodness, we used to call them hippies in my day, ha ha ha…Paul, you are looking soooooooooooo thin, are you eating?"

"Eating? What's that?" He said,

She laughed and smacked him in the back of the head, which pissed him off and gave Darryl a grin and a chuckle –

"Paul, honey, go in the kitchen, in the cupboards above the fridge…"

"Which cupboard?"

"The one with the picture of the naked chick pole dancing…"

"Lovely…"

"There are a few cartons of cigarettes in there, you kids can have a pack each, ok?"

"Alright…"

Paul made his way to the kitchen while Darryl and Mom laughed and smoked and drank and ate their sandwiches – he looked around and saw the naked chick on the cupboard then he saw the bread box which he remembered his mom used to store extra cash, he paused…then he peered into the living room…Darryl and his mom were laughing and having a ball…he thought about it…looked inside, there were some loose bills, maybe 50 or 60 bucks…he put it all in his pocket and started for the living room but on the way saw the paint peeling off one of the hallway walls, the kitchen floor stained and forgotten, the cupboards all pockmarked and scarred – he remembered running around this house as a kid when for a brief moment everyone was happy…he went to the kitchen, put the  money back, grabbed three packs of smokes from the cupboard and rejoined the party –

..............................................................

"Why didn't you ask her for money, man?" Said Darryl as he lit a joint, took a puff and passed it to Paul -

"C'mon dude, did you see her? She's broke – drunk – couldn't do it, man…"

"Yeah, okay, I hear ya, dude, I always dug your mom…does she sleep in that chair in front of the T.V?"

"Don't know if she ever gets out of it…"

"Well alright…let's go get that shit that Cracker owes us…maybe we can sell it in time for the show, or something…"

"Better yet…we'll ask him for cash instead of the weed, how's that?"

"You are brilliant, dude, brilliant!"

"That's why the call me "the bum"!"

"I never heard anyone call you that…"

"Well they do…"

"But it doesn't even make sense…*the bum*…what the fuck does it mean?"

"Don't worry about it, asshole, let's go!"

"I'm going, watch me!"

They reached Cracker's house in about 20 minutes walking through the dingy neighborhood smell of factory smoke and laid-down drunks and bad-habit school teachers then past the factory-wreckage and into the tree-lined overworked streets and the smell of grass deep and green everywhere making you forget for a second that this was a shitty place full of tired people that had given up and been laid to rest in front of their televisions, they both wore beatle boots and the clicking sound on the sidewalk echoed through the dangerously quiet neighborhood and it started to make Paul nervous – they stopped…

"Doesn't look like anyone's home…" Said Darryl,

House all dark and ugly and charred front lawn grey and dismal not a sound anywhere,

"He hangs out in the basement, remember?"

"Doesn't he live with his grandmother?"

"Yeah, but she's almost deaf…let's go to the back, that's the basement entrance…"

They went through the front yard and to the rear tripping over rakes, hoses, rocks, overgrown grass, what the hell, then they knocked on the back door – without their noticing Cracker came up quietly behind them,

"FUCKERS!"

They jumped out of their skin and he laughed,

"What the fuck, dude!" Said Darryl,

"I was sitting out here in back, heard you guys from 10,000 miles away, ha ha ha ha…let's go inside…"

They went through the back door ducking into the low ceiling and straight down the stairs, but then Cracker's grandmother shouted from somewhere deep inside,

"WHO WANTS COOKIES?"

"Ah, c'mon man" Said Paul, "I don't want to see your grandmother, I'm too baked…"

"Well you have to try the homemade cookies man, chocolate chips, fucking to die for…"

"Yeah, Paul, what the fuck's wrong with you? We have to try the cookies!" Said Darryl,

So they went upstairs and the old lady stood there tray in hand and the cookies smelling like heaven but she was old and frail and somewhat out of her mind and Paul felt a wave of sadness come over him – Darryl on the other hand was shoving cookies down his mouth like it was the end of civilization with Cracker smiling proudly in the back eyes glazed over and deadly,

"Let's go downstairs, c'mon, dude, hurry up" Said Cracker

They followed him down and Paul took one last look back as the old lady just stood there sad smile on her face all lost and alone and so near the end, basement was large self-contained apartment washroom, kitchen, bedroom, living room black and white pics all over the walls of movie stars, musicians, naked people, athletes, guns and rifles and tanks and war-planes and bombed-out European cities after the war, dust and spider webs collected in corners old Fender Tele sat on a stand beside a stereo and a turntable and a very impressive album collection that circled the room hugging the baseboards everything you could want was there from rock and roll to jazz to blues to reggae from 1960 to 1989 – any music that came out after the 80's was not allowed in his house…

"Good music died in 1989, motherfuckers…" He said as he put on Chemicrazy from That Petrol Emotion and lit a big fat joint puffing and passing it around, hear the needle scratch the vinyl and that beautiful violent sound invade the room and their minds and they sat and listened cross-legged around the large round marble coffee-table covered in rolling papers and buds of deep green pot with red strands interwoven, empty packs of Du Maurier cigarettes were all over the floor and table and a few full ones sat in front of Cracker,

"Yeah…(puff puff) this is a great band…you guys going to the show tonight?"

"Well that's why we're here, Cracker – y'see -

"I like the way the guitars overlap through the whole record…you hear it?"

"Yeah, it's fucking awesome!" said Darryl, "Paul thinks Babble is their best record…cray, right, man…"

"It's just more involved, you know? Right Cracker?" Said Paul,

"More involved hell! It's just weirder, that's all…" Said Darryl,

"Why does everything have to be fucking easy for you? Easy music, easy job, or NO job, easy chicks, huh? Why?"

"And why do you have to always prove how fucking smart you are, *'oh, lookit me, I like complicated music, I listen to Babble'*…"

"I'm not being anything, dickwad…"

"Shitface!"

"Enough - assholes!" Said Cracker –

"Okay, listen man, remember that shit you owe us?" Said Paul,

"What shit?"

"That shit…we moved it for you, remember?"

"I don't know what you're talking about, man?"

"Cracker, c'mon man" Said Darryl, "You said if we moved that shit for you, you'd give us an O.Z.….that night, Suzy's party?"

"Suzy's party….that was a blur – great fucking night!" He laughed,

"Okay, so you remember us moving all that shit for you, right?" Said Paul,

Cracker kept quiet –

Paul and Darryl looked at each other –

"You trying to rip us off, dude?" Said Paul looking right at Cracker –

"Yeah, buddy…" Said Darryl menacingly–

The album ended – the tension rose – it was quiet –

Cracker got up and started to slowly move to a corner –

"Look, man, we're not leaving here without that O.Z. or cash" Said Paul as he and Darryl stood up,

"Yeah, what he said…" Said Darryl tough and ready,

Cracker sped up sensing trouble his tattered bathrobe falling loose and his balls hanging out for a second but suddenly out of a drawer he had a gun in his hands casually holding it and waving it around the room,

"Whoa…" Said Darryl,

"What the fuck, man, easy, buddy, easy…" Said Paul –

"So…what do I owe you, assholes?" Said Cracker moving around the room with that fucking death-machine in his hand all bright and shiny and ready,

"Okay, okay, man, we're out of here…you don't owe us shit…"

They went up the stairs slowly till Cracker pointed the gun at them then they bolted out the door into the streets and kept running and running hearing Grandma shouting, "COOKIES, COOKIES!" Fading into distance and hot night -

"What the fuck….what the fuck!" Said Paul bent over catching his breath,

"What a fucking ass-wipe!"

"He ain't getting away with this…fuck!..asshole!"

"You bet he ain't…"

Darryl pulled something out of his inside pocket –

"Check it out, baby!"

And there it was – a goddamn pile of grass in a half-torn paper bag, all beautiful and green and red and at least 2 or 3 ounces of it –

"HOLY SHIT, MAN!" Said Paul, then he laughed and laughed, and they laughed and they laughed, and nothing else was heard on those streets among the trees and silent gutter-alleys,

"How…when the fuck?" Said Paul,

"As soon as we got there, man…that's what that fucker was doing in the yard…"

"What do you mean, dude?"

"He was hiding shit…but he's always wasted, so he fucks up…this bag was sitting right beside the garage…when you guys went in, I grabbed it…"

"You are a fucking God, man!"

"Shit, if the bag didn't rip, we would have a lot more…"

"Okay, what now? What time is it….okay, 9 o'clock…at least 2 hours till That Petrol Emotion comes on…let's –

"- Sell that shit and move the fuck on!"

And they went straight for the concert 3 bus rides and eager-waiting then the ghetto flying by the window with all the bag ladies and homeless wonders and garbage piled up high and the loose-cannon freewheeling outsiders on street corners smiling crooked and knowing everything, and there were kids on stolen bikes with burned-out back lights and their smiles large and beautiful dragged by their hearts into all of this tragically hip beat-down, and nothing ever happens – and nothing ever changes – and nothing ever gives a damn –

Then they were there, large crowd in front, music coming from inside all the 20-somethings hanging loose and cool with their beards and goatees and pointy shoes and smoking imported cigarettes and the smell of good grass in the chill-easy night, chicks in jean shorts, chicks in black tights and dock martins, chicks in tight jeans and bright red pumps, everyone smiling and waiting for the band and that golden moment to come again, smiles spread on Paul and Darryl's face and the goosebumps travelled from head to toe and they were there – they were home –

"Alright, dickie-boy" Said Paul as they approached the crowd, "Get ready to sell your ass…"

"Dickie-boy? What the fuck?"

"Just get ready –

"But what the fuck does it even mean – dickie-boy?"

"That you're a dickhead, get it, ass-fuck?"

"Maybe I don't, ass-wipe!"

"Just get ready!"

'I'm ready as hell!"

And it went well, and they sold, they sold by eye, nothing weighed, nothing measured, just a free-for-all magic-carpet-ride, and they got high, and they popped some pills, and they bought some booze, and they got drunk fast and easy and lovely, and soon it was time as they bought tickets from the front door and prepared to lock it up nice and tight standing outside the cabaret summer night feeling long and warm and the city lights framing everything in golden orange and Paul commenting on how bright the night felt, brighter than the sun said Darryl, they shook hands, a quick hug,

what a day said Paul smiling –

The sound all around them, the music, the laughter, the thrill to be alive,

yeah, said Darryl, what a trip man –

the best…you're the best, dude –

I hear ya…you're my main dude, know what I'm saying, bro  –

   At that moment a white van turned the corner bringing all its evil intentions right at them and Cracker sat in the passenger seat gun in his hand and big bald motherfucker with red goatee at the wheel, they moved forward slowly approaching and something clicked into place, and something paused, and something went wild and crazy, and the city moved forward without concern or care Paul bright and always merry under the golden night-lights…

# 110 IN THE SHADE

Listenin' to Sonny Boy Williamson smoking grass and playing guitar along with the tunes trying to figure out that blues-riffin' got the lead parts down but rhythm giving me a hard time, just listen old boy, give it your ear, give it your guts, give it your feeling and all else let the pick kinda groove over the strings like they're made out of water, here it comes, yeah that's it –

So I got it, I got it figured and playing in groove with Sonny Boy is alright, feeling alright guitar in my hands and on my lap vibrating in time and out, and I know what it means right at that moment cuz with eyes shut and ears alive and wide open it tells me "you go man, you go baby!" I'm ripping a few leads feeling it to my very bones then back to rhythm I go and I am alone, and I feel alone, and I feel great, let me tell ya, it's all just a gas, it's all just for kicks, postcards from Paris after an easy sunrise, then tune changes to Lou Reed's Rock and Roll Animal, ooooh yeah, this calls for something different, man, I'm telling ya –

Now I have to treat the strings like they're made out of barbwire, gotta kiss them with violence, song easy to play, easy to feel, song is back-alley brilliant so c'mon and let me know baby, Lou Reed telling me something cool and angry and it ain't just for kicks brother he's saying, it's for violent ass-whoopins' drinking Spumante and Whiskey Sours with mud-laced dock martins sweating all over, alright then asshole, I say, and I turn my amp up, and I get it, right then and there, I get it going mean lean hungry bastard –


My wife Izzy walks into the room while I'm playing to The Sensational Alex Harvey Band head down trying to get those fingers running up those strings and you gotta be pissed playing guitar to this shit man, you gotta spit it out with no-mercy anger, you gotta mean it with no bullshit allowed 110 in the shade, ya dig?


She stands and stares and listens – she's in underwear and a t-shirt – she's beyond beautiful – half-bottle of Rye on coffee table and Vambo Marble Eye running to the rescue, he's screaming and pointing a well-manicured hand at me and saying with fury-rock and roll, "you go man, you go baby!" and she joins in cuz she's been waitin' just for this moment in all the coma-altered watered down opinions "do that that thing" she says, "what thing" I say, "that thing we like" she says crying and singing and telling God that it ain't nothing old man -

And the punk-rock wandering in the cemetery is as alive as it ever
was –


Making the rent next month, however, and getting the trash cans
out on the curb for Monday morning is still a problem -

# SEX ON A TRAIN

Train a-rollin' I was staring out the back window as the station got smaller and smaller and my mother and grandmother waving at me looking oh so sad and eventually a bell rang and they were gone – train bolted through Torino in northern Italy past the ancient cobblestone and long-stretch highways and monuments of yester-year and the damn thing shook and rattled and everything felt like an electric flash of something wild going through my head, I was 13 years old, 1978 or 79, and the times were loose and groovy and there were marijuana-mindscapes rubbing the streets clean – I had just moved back to Italy the country of my birth for the third time after living in Canada for most of my childhood but this time the old man and older brother had stayed behind for reasons unclear to me and as soon as I got to the airport my mother and grandmother and uncle looking gloom-doom cryin' brought me to train station in downtown Torino explaining in Italian that my cousins, aunts and uncles were waiting and that it would be two weeks on the Italian Riviera apartment complex right on the beach, but why I said? Just a vacation, mother replied all grim and sad and droopy, so I thought, fine with me, fucking ay!

Now don't be scared alone on the train said mother, oh no, said grandmother, no no, don't be scared, just stay in open compartments and in plain view of staff, they all know about you and they will be looking out for you - not scared, I said and scrambled up onto the train and waved away, and away, and away – so there I was alone– we were leaving Torino and Piazza Nuova and Via Roma and Corso Unione Sovietica and Lo Stadio Comunale and Il Palazzo Valentino all behind us in a big blur of nothing and the land moved swiftly past my eyes I saw valleys, I saw small towns, I glimpsed mountains, saw farmers in their fields, saw rivers and taverns and the towns were attached one after another, and people smiled and cursed, and the young women looked incredible to my 13 year old virgin eyes and there were truck-stops and gas-bars and the train stopped and I got off and bought a sandwich of prosciutto and provolone cheese, then back in compartment with door open and a steady stream of people going back and forth, couples loving, couples arguing, young men just cruising the country looking for shit to do, family of three young girl and elderly parents sat with me hurtling insults at each other (little girl included) just to pause, smile, and talk to me interested and friendly then a sudden burst from one of them and off they went again, little girl jumping around cabin like a monkey, parents shouting, myself confused and a little afraid all shit breaking loose but suddenly train announced our arrival to Milano, wow, they got off in a hurry and all so polite and happy and little girl kissing me on the cheek and the parents winking and smiling off they went – good riddance I said to myself –

Nothing to see outside but grey platform and people running around like idiots messing up their lives everyone smoking cigarettes, cigarettes in their mouths, in their fingers, under their heels, people were all lit up and ready to go nowhere at all, but I suddenly spotted something unbelievable – this young woman somewhere in her 20's walked right by with long red hair and blue eyes and bell-bottom jeans tight around the ass and thighs and I watched her shoving my head out the window and arching my neck out of position as much as humanly possible – out of view I could hear her talk and get on the train – I sat still – I heard footsteps, high heels come down the hall, closer and closer then she walked right into the compartment smiling and putting her luggage up top and sitting right across from me – she started talking immediately in proper Italian and after my initial nervousness I replied and it was cool, she seemed kind and considerate and when she laughed and crossed her legs I glanced at her thighs wondering what they looked like bare, and we passed the town of Pavia and now you could see the mountains plainly and the colors of the country went from green to purple and orange and the sun was shining up high coming through the window in a bright flash of beautiful Sunday – she kept lighting cigarettes one after the other and I noticed a young man with a thin mustache and baggy pants kept walking by our compartment and that her smile would fade when she saw him only to come back as crazy-beautiful as ever red lips and toes painted aquamarine she wore leather sandals with small heels, what a broad, man, Jesus Christ! But we kept talking – and after a while we even went silent and just stared out the window as the third hour of the trip rode up on us and we reached a city called Bologna my friend excusing herself,

"Watch my bags, okay?" She said big smile winking, "I'll be right back"

"Sure thing"

So I strained my neck out the window trying to see where this broad was going but nothing happening rest of platform hopping with all sorts of action long-haired hippies standing alone and in groups in sandals or boots with tie-dyed smiles and easy expectations, and the short-hair dudes with long sideburns in their casual shirts dress pants slick zipper boots all groovy and ready their gals running up hugging kissing and jostling for attention, and there were kids running around jumping and hollering excited about something or just really digging being alive while their parents frowned and puffed and blew out uneasy air, be happy I thought to myself, why not be happy you old fools, I mean in the end we're just dirt in the ground so why not be happy while ya still can, right? But the parents always seeming the most miserable to me, ain't ever having kids I thought, no damn way baby, I could smell food cooking and I saw beer being drank and I felt the hot breeze coming in from the window and my long hair trailing out and around me, thought I heard some music coming from somewhere an electric guitar doing something wild and crazy, but then, holy shit, there she was talking to that guy with the thin mustache and baggy pants they seemed to be fighting and she quietly snapped her neck around and her thick red hair did something beautiful, and he sort of listened and smiled crooked and all-greasy blue-jean-blues right around the corner, train about to leave saw her run off and in she came heard the heels coming my way and the train goes a-whistling once again and once again those tracks start rolling and there we went, tap tap tap go those heels she walked in and sat across from me face flush from anger more beautiful than before she looked at me, smiled, looked out window, back at me, anger subsiding her eyes grinned brand new,

"So how are you?" She said,

"Fine...how about you?"

"I'm alright...so when did you get back from Canada? Oh, I have some food -  couple of sandwiches, some salad...you want some?"

"No, that's alright..."

"So what was I saying....oh yeah, when did you get here?"

"This morning..."

"Wow...straight from a plane to a train...why the rush, I mean..."

"I don't know...I got off the plane...my mom and grandmother and uncle were there and they said I was going to see my other uncle and cousins in Rimini...that's all I know...my dad and brother stayed back in Canada this time...don't know why..."

"Oh..." She looked sad suddenly -

"Well, there's nothing wrong with them...my parents...I mean, they're not getting divorced or anything..."

"Oh no, of course not...you know, I haven't asked you your name..."

"Well, everyone calls me Ziggy…"

"…okay…"

"You can call me Ziggy too…you know…what's yours?"

"Lucy…"

She pulled a beer out of her bag cracked it open taking a long swig then offered me some,

"Well, I've never had beer…what's it taste like?"

"It's good – here…"

"I'm not 18…"

"No shit" She laughed,

"Isn't it illegal?"

"Not in Italy…maybe in Canada…"

"You mean, I kid can drink beer if he wants?"

"And buy it too…my nephew buys me wine from the corner store all the time…"

"Okay…let me try…"

She passed me the bottle – her fingers touched mine and I felt a surge – then the beautiful moment passed – I took a small sip –

"Ugggg, don't like it…sorry…" I said almost gagging,

"Ha ha ha ha ha ha, no problem…you'll love it in a few years…"

"Yeah…"

Our door open I saw people walking by our cabin continually looking in smiling moving on happily some looking grim and dour –

"So…do you have a girlfriend?"

"I did…in Canada…"

"Where do you like it better, Italy or Canada?"

"Canada…I spent more time there, you know?"

"Oh, really?"

"Yeah…I already miss it…"

Lucy looked at her watch nervously fidgeting about and rolling her eyes and smiling sadly looking out window looking out cabin door looking at me people in hall thinning out and train feeling quiet and distant, and we were rolling through the province of Ravenna farmland stretching far and wide small wooden cabins lined with trees and Via Corletta running alongside of us sky hanging over everything pure and blue and simple reminded me of Winnipeg back in Canada that prairie land moving out in front of you begging you to follow its grind and moan and broken down rhythm to its bitter and sad-happy end, goddamn I missed it and I suddenly realized it was gone, damn, gone for good, I missed hanging out at the corner store, I missed drinking coca cola in the junkyard with my friends of all races, I missed walking the neighborhoods with the tall tree-lined streets overlapping up top bringing shade to the streets, there was no fighting it, I was born in Italy but I felt Canadian, I breathed Canadian, I lived in groove with that Canadian rhythm, that Canadian way of living and thinking, ain't no doubt about it, what the hell was I doing here I thought, what the hell!

"I'll be right back" Said Lucy anxiously, looking at her watch –

"Okay…"

She was gone suddenly and it was real quiet and the time passed and I could see a sliver of ocean in the distance following the train as it curved its way down the Italian railroad, the city of Cesena flew right by looking flat and green and rural saw a cemetery and the sun glistening off the grey tombstones and the dead grinning like they finally knew it all, Lucy was missing for quite a while, a good hour or so, so I left the compartment to stretch my legs walking the tight corridor out among the greasy earthlings all seeming sad and lonely went from one section to the next to the next and to a very quiet one with hardly anyone there – a young lady sat alone by a window – middle aged man read a book with feet up and head on pillow – then no one – started hearing sounds like someone crying – moaning – paused, then went closer – now it was two voices – male and female – reached compartment, door closed but small window on front – the sounds were loud and clear now, two people fucking – I was a virgin but I knew the sounds from movies and heard my aunt and uncle once as I slept over for the week-end in downtown Milan – I looked behind me – no one there – I took a look – naked man and woman tightly entwined sitting up against a chair– man's back was facing me and woman's head buried in his shoulders – they moved side to side and up and down and grabbed each other tight making crying sounds – I darted and moved back a few paces…wow…couldn't believe my eyes…I inched forward as quiet as shit and looked in – they knocked the chair over and fell to the ground and without missing a beat kept going at it…I felt something happening in my jeans…I watched in awe, a bit grossed out, a bit turned-on…then I saw the red hair and I saw Lucy...and the guy with her was pencil mustache, his baggy pants strewn on the floor...she had her head tilted back and her mouth was wide open barely making a sound and I kept looking and they kept fucking and I suddenly felt very sad - then she saw me through the window over the guy's shoulder – our eyes met – she held them in place – then closed them and went back at it again with renewed fervor – her legs were high in the sky and my eyes began to focus on one of her thighs all big and pearl-white and glistening wet and she kept it there hanging in the air and I could see her painted toes aquamarine and shining and the screams got louder and louder and the announcement rang through the entire train, RIMINI, TOWN OF RIMINI, train slowing down to a crawl I glanced out the side window saw my uncle and aunt and young cousins standing on the platform waiting, looked back in Lucy on floor legs spread far and wide, got flashes of us talking in our compartment, her smile and crossed legs and her eyes big and blue, didn't seem like same person down on ground, didn't seem it at all, caught a glimpse of the ocean outside the window, there were ripples on its surface as the wind said something wild and the smell of coconut oil filled the air...

# THE BARBER

They wandered the hallway going in and out of each other's rooms. They were in a locked unit. The hall was 100 feet straight with sudden turns at each end and doors with combination locks and alarms. The nurses hung around listlessly, and the doctors were absent and uninterested, and the receptionists were never at their desks - this is all the wanderers had, this was their entire world, Alzheimer's took everything else.

Marie came every day to see her father and for the last two the small garbage can in his room was full of piss. She tied the plastic bag that sat at the bottom of the can and threw it into a bin. She looked down the hall and there wasn't a nurse in sight – just the zombies walking back and forth mumbling and cursing and looking incredibly unhappy. One guy was black and he would sit at a window having a phone conversation into his empty hand, going into great detail. Another was a small white guy about 80 years old who walked around swearing his head off and growling at whoever crossed his path. A lady in a wheelchair pulled herself down the hall by the handicapped bar that hugged the walls only to stop, examine the bar with great interest, then continue. A few watched T.V. in the common room and laughed and howled and commented to each other even though the set was broken and hadn't been turned on in years. They all shit and pissed in their pants, in the closets, in buckets and pails, in the hallway, everywhere but in the toilets.

It was straight out of Kesey's "Cuckoo Nest" – these people were trapped, in their heads, and in this prison-hospital.

Marie's father had advanced Alzheimer and he only recognized her half the time at best. But he seemed to derive some pleasure from her visits as his mood brightened when she came by. Maybe deep in his subconscious he still knew her - maybe deep in his subconscious he was still who he had always been.

He laid on the bed and talked nonsensically without pause, but he also laughed and giggled and acted like a kid who had just gotten out of school, happy with no conscious knowledge of the world and all its shit – finally he got tired and laid on the bed, closed his eyes, and moaned off and on punctuated by the one same phrase he always said while between sleep and wakefulness – "I didn't mean to do it – "

Maries looked at him running her hand through his hair and the tears fell down her cheeks – then she remembered, she remembered...


........................................................................

Every day at 7 AM sharp Mario opened his barber shop and let the light in. He had been doing this for 35 years. It was the great pleasure of his life. It's what he did back in the old country, and it was the only thing he wanted to do. The shop was on Main Street at the very beginning of skid row. Right beside it was the first barfly hotel of many more that lined the street on either side. The bell above the door rang and in walked the first customer.

"John you crazy kid!" Said Mario in a thick Italian accent,

"Only you would call a 50 year old a kid…but keep it coming, keep it coming…"

"Sit down, sit down…"

John sat in the middle barber chair and Mario flung that apron around him like it was a bullfighter's cape –

"How are things at work, my friend?" Said Mario,

"They suck…10 more years and I can retire, 10 more fucking years!…take your time, Mario, I'm not in any rush to go back…"

John worked across the street at an Opera House as the head janitor. He only worked week-ends. There was hardly anyone in the building and he could basically do whatever he wanted. After the haircut he would go back, mop the lobby, then go to the rehearsal room in the basement and play his trumpet. He was a jazz musician for a local band – it was his main thing and they were quite good, and they played around town a lot, but, as in most arts, you're either rich or poor – he fell in with the latter.

"How's the wife, Mario?"

"The wife is a pain in the ass, as usual…"

He stood behind John looking in the mirror and measuring things like an artist at his canvas.

"And your daughter, what's her name - Conchetta?"

"Where the hell did you get that? It's Marie – my little girl is the light of life…"

"I would have thought this place took that honor…"

"Well, maybe she is second…ha ha ha ha ha"

"She still married?"

"Yes, yes, they are very happy…"

"So how is this different than your shop in Italy?"

He sprayed the back of John's head with a water bottle and the scissors started clicking. In the background a small transistor radio played AM hits from the 70's.

"Well, first of all, look out there…"

He pointed at the window. There were two foot snow banks lining the sidewalks and the wind was blowing hard at the window.

"Outside my window in Italy there was a cobblestone road with cafes that led to the beach and palm trees and people getting drunk on the sand…all year long…"

"I see your point…"

"In Italy, the stores, they open whenever they want…people relax and don't make problems about it…if they are closed, they come back later…here, if you are closed, you lose customers to the next guy and you starve…"

"Why did you come here, Mario?"

"Well, in Italy you reach a point, and you never can move up…here, you can make money, you can buy a house, you can move up…I love Italy, it is my country…but a better life for Marie is here…"

He continued to trim John's gray hair with great pride and precision. The bell rang at the door and it opened bringing the freezing wind inside. In walked a young Native fellow with a bag in hand.

"Hey Ivan, how are you?" Said Mario, "Come in, sit down…"

"Alright, Pops - how's it hanging, John, how's the music?"

"Rock and roll my friend…"

Ivan moved around and sat right beside John.

"What you have in there?" Said Mario to Ivan,

"Well, I've got some brand new jeans, only 5 dollars a pop…"

"Girl's?"

"What you mean?"

"Girl's or boy's jeans?"

"Well they're good for either, everything is good for either these days, Pops…"

"I cannot tell boys from girls anymore, John, I can't…"

"I know what you mean, man…here, Ivan let me see them…"

So they look at the jeans, complain, argue, agree, and Ivan leaves with a few more bucks in his pockets than he came in with. Mario hugged him and gave him the usual stern talk about staying away from gangs and crime and drugs, and so on….

"You know he's going to get high now, right?" Said John,

"Maybe...but I think it is only marijuana...if it stays there, it's okay, no?"

"Couldn't live without my green, that's for sure..."

He stretched back in the chair and Mario continued.

"Look at those drunks outside, man, it's only 10 in the morning – how the hell have you dealt with it all these years?"

"They are not bad people – most of them – they are lost, John, that's all...if they cause problems, I kick their ass down the street, you know that..."

"I've got no patience for people pissing their lives away, it's a bloody waste..."

"Yeah, well, it is their life, not ours..."

"Oh shit, they're coming right up to your window, Mario..."

In a flash, Mario was out the door and sending them on their way – he was a tough ol' boy from Southern Italy with that short, stocky, round gut, powerful build, and this shit was nothing to him.

"Y'see?" He said to John proudly,

"You the man, Mario, you the man..."

"And the haircut is done...."

"Once again, you've outdone yourself..."

John paid him and they sat at the front counter drinking coffee and looking out the window. It was almost deserted outside with the occasional drunk stumbling by. Not a single sober person walked down that street on Sunday mornings. They were scavenging for cigarette butts, lost money, food, clothes, all of last night's leftovers.

"Let's go in the back" Said Mario "I'll make you a real coffee…"

They went through the door and into a room with a table and a few chairs around it. There was also a counter with an Espresso maker on it. A bottle of Cognac was right beside it. John pointed to the machine and smiled.

"You better fucking believe I want one of those…" He said –

Mario made two Espressos and poured a shot of Cognac in each.

"This is called Caffe Coretto in Italian – you have it in the morning just before your day starts."

"So the "Coretto" part means you add booze to it?"

"Yes…"

"Man, you can't beat that…"

They drank it and continued talking, old friends happy to be in each other's company. The front door bell went off again. Mario peaked out the back room.

"Ciro! Vieni dentro, vieni!" He said,

It was an old Italian friend from little Italy where they lived. They had known each other for thirty years.

"Ciao, ciao – what is happening today? Ciao, John, how are you?"

"Living the dream, Ciro, living the dream…"

"Espresso?" Asked Mario,

"I would not hate you if you made me a cup…"

"Coretto?"

"Why the hell not, huh, that's what I say…"

They sat and watched him drink for a second – there was a deck of old Italian cards on the table and Ciro stared playing around with them as they talked.

"How about a game of Scopa?" He said,

"Is that the one where you have to match up the cards? The 7 of Gold, the Horseman, all that shit?"

"That is the one, you ignorant American…" Laughed Mario,

"Canadian…"

"What the hell is the difference, deal the shit…" Said Ciro,

Slow day at the barber shop as they kept playing cards and drinking coffee. Then they gave up the coffee and kept the Cognac going. They played and laughed and Mario would break into Neapolitan folk songs and Ciro would join in and John was digging the whole thing. Not a single customer, not a single worry, said Mario – well into the morning they went, then into the afternoon.

"Ever seen the shit that happens down the street here at night?" Said John,

"It's a never-ending parade." Said Mario,

"People are drunk and high…and fucking mean….man, it's some grim stuff…"

"Hookers everywhere…" Said Mario -

"That's the good part" Laughed Ciro in that thick Neapolitan accent, intensely happy to be alive -

"I saw a guy once charging cars with a fucking stop sign right down Main Street, and I mean those big fucking steel things that sit at street corners, not those little hand-held things…" Said John,

"Really?" Said Ciro,

"Oh yeah, it was 3 in the morning, I was working the night shift eating my lunch at the big windows facing Main Street….he was running against traffic, cars swerving and crashing, all that shit…"

"Like a mediaeval knight, the hell with it, death to everyone!"

"I remember in Italy" Said Mario, "after dinner, everybody went for a walk, everywhere in the country, people walking, talking, laughing, arguing, it was a custom...not like here, eat, then sit on the couch drink beer and watch television..."

"In Napoli, they have the best Gelato in the world, you could kill someone for it...sitting at the piazza, looking at the girls...huh..." Said Ciro -

"What a beautiful city! I have been there many times!"

"Yes, you know what they say - see Napoli, then die..."

"That's nothing man, you should see the chicks at my jazz gigs...women will do anything for a man who plays an instrument..." Said John -

The front bell rang and they heard the door open and the cold wind flood the room. Mario went to the front room and there she stood – 5'8", blonde, stacked, curvy, green eyes like the devil in heels –

"Mario, how are you?"

"Stacy, one second dear…"

He told the fools in the back to carry on, he had business, then winked – they peaked out and saw Stacy, smiled and dealt the cards, had another drink as Ciro started singing.

"Stacy my friend, where have you been?" Said Mario beckoning her to a chair,

"Just busy with life and all that shit, you know…"

"Yes, sometimes, all of that shit can drive you crazy…in Italy we enjoy our life and live for the moment and sing and dance…"

"Really, it's just like that?"

"No, not really…but in some places, at certain times…"

"Give me the usual my friend…"

He began with the shampoo tilting her head back gently and lathering it up, feeling every moment. Stacy had blonde hair all the way down to her ass and it was thick and healthy. In almost 40 years of marriage Mario had never cheated on his wife, not once – but he allowed himself this without guilt. He ran his hands through that hair and he felt cool and easy and slightly turned on - so it went on – and on – and the songs and laughter from the back kept coming, and Stacy dug it all, and she smiled and talked and looked into the mirror. Then it was done. The song 'Leroy Brown' from the 70's was in full bloom on the radio.

"Mario, you outdid yourself – beautiful!"

She paid him and left and Mario watched her leave with a sigh and a sad smile. Then he locked the door and ran to the back –

"Deal me in, shitheads!"

Few hours later they were all drunk and happy and were deciding on what next –

"Man, I gotta go check in at work, how the fuck am I going to do this?" Laughed John,

"With great pride and a lot of bullshit" said Ciro –

"Go on, kid" said Mario, "I got to get Marie to come pick us up, we are too drunk for the car…the wife is going to be pissed, ha ha ha ha ha…did you pay me for the haircut?"

They shook hands and John went out the door, across the street and in to The Opera House. In all the years he had worked there, all 20 of them, the boss had never come in on the week-end – but there he was – and John was fired on the spot.

Mario was on the phone with his daughter, Marie, and was cajoling for a ride –

"C'mon, Marie, we need a lift, just come down…and don't tell your mother!"

"Well why did you have to get drunk in the afternoon?" Said Marie,

"Because I am alive!"

Ciro went into song and they both started laughing. Marie tried to remain serious but chuckled and agreed to pick them up. They went outside and lit cigarettes in the winter night. They saw Ivan across the street in a bus-shack passing a bottle back and forth with a few street-junkies. Ivan waived. They waved back. Just as they were finishing the cigarettes, Marie showed up. She got out trying to be stern but couldn't hide her amusement. They got in and the car slid on the ice, gained its balance and moved forward....

...................................................................................

Mario the barber laid in bed asleep and mumbling sadly. Marie, his daughter, held him and whispered in his ear. The pressure of taking care of her father had ended her marriage. The barber shop was sold some time ago. Outside the room the sound of the fellow on his imaginary phone could be heard mingled with all the other lost and sad voices. Marie's mother stood in the doorway. She held two coffees in hand. She went to her daughter and handed her one of the cups then sat beside her. Then she took Mario's hand. The night continued after that....

# TEENAGE FREAK-OUT

It was my third time running away from home each time being about two or three months long ending with the old man finding me hanging out on some street corner or another, so don't know if you could call it "running away" but in my mind every time was the final time and every time was permanent and every time was the great escape, but anyway – the first time I had slept in a park under a bush for a few weeks, second time I slept on the roof of my high school, third time at the bottom of the stairs of an apartment block in our neighborhood, this time I was holed up in a shack part of an abandoned lot with the house torn down and only this small garage-type thing made out of rotten wood still standing on a patch of worn-out grass but place rather clean inside and I leaned up with my back to the walls arms around legs smoking cigarettes a friend had given me and just thinking about anything that came to my head and about the fact that this shack was right across the street and a few houses down from my place, I could see the front door, the grey steps and steel railings, the large living room window, even the address 1129 Waller Street, I could see this from

the cracks in the wood and I found it comical, and I found it tragic
-

Not much of a getaway, I thought about how many of my heroes had jumped steam boats headed for Africa, hitched rides across the country, ran away with the circus, sold machine guns to freedom fighters, stowed away to Paris and slept on park benches and on friend's couches just to be artists, hmmmm, bunch of assholes, I thought, typical and predictable, they ain't me, I ain't them, and I would trade blows with any of them, so I just sat there thinking and smoking when I heard the footsteps outside, heard the rustling of leaves and the clanging of bottles a female cough and I opened the door,

"Cindy..." I said,

"That's how you get in here....quite a place, are you renting or buying?"

"Funny, here, sit down...move those leaves over there...what's in the bag?"

She moved over to a corner with those tight jeans shaking teenage cellulite just right, those round thighs and bubblebut-ass and long hair with bangs cut straight just above big brown eyes, her jean jacket had rips and her runners were blue adidas with the white stripes and she sat down all sweet and pretty and juicy,

"Ziggy" She said, "I've got some performance art right here, three-dimensional art - "

She pulled out a bottle of Southern Comfort - "One - "

Then a 6-pack of beer, stubby bottles - "Two -"

"And the final dimension - " A tiny triangle of paper with a beautiful orange phoenix drawn on it,

"You into some acid?"

"You bet I am..."

She placed it on my tongue then started sucking on her own this being about the 10th time we dropped acid together and it always felt fresh and new and right-on, passing the bottle back and forth we waited for the whole dance to kick in...

"So where are the rest of the do-nothing boys?" I said,

"Don't know, everyone's kind of doing their own thing tonight...Ross and Nazzie are at an out of town party, Brenda and Joe are having sex...Max has some family shit going on...just us, honky..."

"Sounds good to me...you like my new pad?"

We started laughing and lit cigarettes -

"You wonder why they wouldn't tear this thing down too...they tore down the house, why leave this shit-shack?" Said Cindy,

"I dig it..."

"So how long is this one lasting?"

"This one?"

"This latest adventure of yours..."

"Oh, shit, who knows...I don't give a fuck..."

"But you're old man seems like an alright guy...my dad's a complete prick..."

"We get along like shit, and one of these days it's going to get ugly...I'd rather get out before it does..."

"Then my friend, you need a plan...you can't just fuck off and go sleep in a shack across the street from your fucking house..."

"I'm gathering myself...thinking...here, have a nice big swig..."

"Don't need you to tell me, man..."

She took a nice swallow of Southern, then she lit a joint -

"I dig what you're doing, Ziggy, I get it...parents suck!"

"Same with school, I'm dropping out..."

"Shit, you'll get kicked out before that, ha ha ha ha..."

"Yeah, most likely...fuck'em..."

"Is that rain?"

"Yeah, love that sound..."

"I think you and Nazzie should get serious about forming a band...you guys are pretty fucking good..."

"We are fucking serious..."

"I mean, *serious* - get organized, get a place to practice, get some other musicians, that kind of serious."

"Yeah, I know, I know..."

"That bar that my friend owns..."

"The one on Mcgillvary Street?"

"Yeah, on the corner of Pembina, he said he'll let you guys play there if you're decent...he doesn't give a shit if you're not eighteen..."

"You told me already...that's a great fucking idea, we should really get it going...start getting some gigs, get some money, an apartment..."

"I'll move in with you..." She came close her lips on mine,

"Sweet, man, sweet..."

We made out for a while feeling each other up over our clothes between whiskey chugs and cigarettes feeling the marijuana high in full force and the alcohol heat moving through our bodies the acid still far away and the rain hitting the ceiling in rhythmic beats bringing the smell of wet grass inside,

"What the fuck?" I said getting up suddenly and moving towards the far wall sending Cindy flying,

"What the fuck is wrong with you?"

"Sorry...is that the old man?"

"What?" Said Cindy moving towards me - "Jesus, it is..."

There he was getting out of his hatchback in the rain with a small Asian woman coming out the other door scurrying towards the house and laughing with their arms around each other,

"Well what the hell, fuck?" I said,

"Looks like the old man's got himself a girlfriend..."

"What an asshole..."

"C'mon, Zigg, your parents have been divorced for a few years now, give him a break..."

"Whatever - I don't give a shit anyway..."

"You feeling the acid yet?"

"Not yet - you sure this is the real shit?"

"Yeah...I mean, I think so..."

"Who'd you get it from?"

"Murray..."

"Murray? He's a fucking rip-off artist, everyone knows that, you know that, Cindy. Why didn't you get it from Jackie?"

"Murray's been getting some good shit lately, better than Jackie's, ask anyone"

"Okay, okay, no problem....let's give it some time...we got tons of booze and pot anyway, who cares, right?"

"Not I...lay down, let me sit on you"

"Yeah, right, with those chubby thighs you might kill me"

"Yeah, right, you love it..."

"You know, when I was a kid, the old man was loud and old-school-tough and we were kind of afraid of him, but he never laid a hand on me, and sometimes he would laugh his ass off with us, hang out...not often, but every once in a while...he was always out playing cards with his Italian buddies, me and my brother at home with my mom...but I never felt like he wouldn't take care of me, you know, like he didn't care about me....I would say that all and all, he was a good father..."

"Well...I mean...doesn't that tell you something? Maybe it's worth working out, you know?"

"Ah shit, the divorce ruined everything...he changed, I changed, my mom changed, my brother...some good things happened, but the father/son thing was fucked from then on..."

"Fuck, you're lucky, my old man was always stern, always mean and pissed off about something...slapped the shit out of me too...fuck him, he's a cop, he's the enemy, right?"

Some time went by us talking and digging each other and feeling alright,

"Do you ever wonder, Cindy....all these moments that we live, all the good times, this moment right here, how fucking fast they move, then, bang, they're gone, just like that...you think they mean anything at all?

"I don't think they mean anything, Ziggy...well, I mean, they don't mean anything except to us, know what I'm saying?"

"I hear ya - you mean that they don't mean anything to the universe, they don't mean anything objectively...but my experiences, the things that matter to me, THAT is my universe, the only one that really exists, so if something means something to me, then it means something - period, you know?"

"I dig, I dig...and as we share experiences, our universes join, making a larger, unified thing, you know - it all comes together in the end, one way or another..."

"We're talking...weird..."

"Like acid, this is acid-talk..."

"Murray, you little prick, you came through"

And then it began...slowly...that feeling in the pit of your guts like something's about to happen like everything is just around the corner, that taste of copper in your mouth, the slight tingling of the scalp, and that glow that starts to circle everything especially people, Cindy moved in close her body rubbing against me and her lips touching mine over and over as we say funny things and the world laughs with us guts bursting, time becomes a fluid thing stopping and starting and flowing and moving in all directions couldn't tell if hours or minutes had passed just Cindy with those big brown eyes seeming innocent and devilish at the same time and we kept talking and laughing and kissing then laughing again as the rain kept hitting the roof harder and harder room all dark with street lights streaming through the cracks in the wood like tight laser beams small round spots hovering on the ground, holy shit man, they're looking for us says Cindy, they're looking for us, shhhhh, I say, shhhhh, it's just the acid talking, go with it, baby, just go with the flow and feel good, who the fuck are you she says, the Maharashi? Wow, had cigarette between lips and bottle of Southern in hand thinking just three years ago I was on a train in Italy going to the Italian Riviera, what the fuck happened, what happened to junkyard Lucy, I was looking out the cracks watching the occasional car fly by in the rain and the water was everywhere I could hear the sound of an ocean and for a second thought we were getting flooded out, watch out, said Cindy, watch out, holy fuck! She dove down in the leaves for cover and it looked like there were a mountain of them and I saw her there messy hair ripped jeans round eyes rounder and a bright yellow glow of light circled her and she looked like a bohemian queen and I dove right in as we rolled around stumbling to get into each other's pants and making out like rock and roll demons in the junkyard, head down I was really going for it, whew,

"Ziggy..."

Huh, what?

"ZIGGY!"

I turned around Cindy standing there looking at me wide eyes mouth screaming,

"What the fuck are you doing?"

I was in a corner on a pile of leaves in the humping position suddenly realizing I had hallucinated fucking Cindy then we started laughing like it was the end of all things and I'm sure they heard us in Russia in France in Turkey and all around the world in Evil Weiner land, could see the lights from my house on across the street then thought about my old man getting it on with his girlfriend and I suddenly felt good for him, I felt happy he was moving on and I told Cindy so proclaiming it like I had discovered everything that ever meant anything, my universe, my glory, Cindy started singing "Soul Kitchen" by The Doors and grooving in the middle of that broken down shack and my broken down life and the acid was in full bloom now and that damn clock in my mind kept running and stopping and rewinding and we started feeling all that groovy shit and violent laughter and righteous bright light feeling just fine and forever, and the hallucinations would creep up on us then move away then sit at the edges and a thousand thrills washed over us and we felt connected to something large and deep,

"I feel it" said Cindy quietly, that no-end-in-sight not ever was all around, it was a drunk-fuck polka dance on the edge of a dying galaxy, it was a sad-night poker game with the devil in drag, it was a Ray Manzarek keyboard solo in a dark kitchen alone and happy, " I feel it", yes indeed, our universes colliding and joining and making us thrill and feel the end absolute, but feel it happily without regret or complaint, the night went on and we finished the bottle but left the beer alone and the come-down part of the trip had just begun and this was the tough part, this was the challenge cuz all that booze and pot and cigarettes and emotional straining suddenly hits you hard in the head and the ride is long and steep and dark and something only the young can endure, so we sat in a corner and held each other nervously watching the shadows on the walls as the cars raced by and the laser beams came through the cracks in the walls in paper-thin strips of high-powered intensity and Cindy's eyes swam in circles...

# I LOVE YOU WHEN YOU'RE DRUNK

There's this coffee shop on the corner of Graham and Kennedy where all the wild ones and the torn and tattered go and the well-dressed too and it's right downtown in the middle of all that shabby thinking and living and I sit here today sipping on hot coffee and steamed milk there's a slow blues song playing, something from T-Bone Walker I believe, they're always playing slow blues and jazz owner an Arab guy, but the blues continue and a guitar solo licks the room and lets it slide and I'm on a stool by a set of very large windows watching the downtown shit as a hobo picks up cigarette butts, an office girl walks briskly along cell phone to her ear and the end-of-summer breeze blowing up her skirt, a food market opens up and the working class welfare crowd start to gather, got one of those Italian biscotti dipping it in the coffee damn thing melts in my mouth feeling like the purpose of all things is right here, group of Africans gather at the corner table every day and talk in their own languages animatedly and passionately, special

needs group comes every morning as well and I really dig the
people that are helping them out and caring for them, here's for
you and all the rest...

Thinking about this book I'm writing, my 17th in 21 years, that is
if you count the 6 chapbooks I wrote at the beginning, all this
writing and publishing and trying to sell the damn things all at my
own cost all losing money all causing grief and great pain and even
greater satisfaction, but you gotta feel all this amazing love running
away with you let me tell ya, life is grand and full of fun-loving
opportunities but learning to spot them is one of the hardest
fucking things to do cuz we're all wrapped up in those bullshit
society things, you know, the gas bill, the light bill, send junior to
school, shitty jobs, mow the lawn, daughter out of control, your
cable is cut off, the snow is piled outside your window, your family
is schizophrenic, weight gain, weight loss, the dog's got fleas, no
money for rent, visits with neighbors you hate, your doctor's gone
fucking nuts, your co-workers are pure evil, the house needs
painting, the apartment has no heat, your girlfriend fucks everyone
but you, your car stalls in winter, standing at the bus-stop in -30
weather, fired from another job you didn't want in the first place,
all things that drag you down down down and get in the way of you
becoming YOU - these things are for the most part unavoidable, I
know, I know, ain't no bleeding heart hippie and I see the world for
what it is, and I see human nature for what it is, but things can be
scaled down and the fat trimmed off, muddy water turned to wine,
ya dig what I'm saying?

But I spill my coffee all over the place goddamn thing goes running down the counter and over the edge, everyone looks at me for a second and owner gives me dirty look and I couldn't care less yet I smile at the guy and he smiles back and the shit is cleaned up and I order another, room is large and long and the people are a steady mix of downtown downtrodden and office workers from nearby high-rises, sky outside looking dark and dirty rain just beginning to fall slow easy and steady like that vulture in your brain and that slinky slide mushroom top in your pants half-ape human drinks mud-stained rum whiskey with dinosaur eggs at midnight, lookie who comes round runnin' down Saskatoon rotten trail groovy sing-sing Tuesday look who cries at sunrise, look who laughs at dawn, look who sprints with Apollo, every day bring-down superstitious diamond scarred alley fucking with a nun, hmmmmmmmmmmmm, this coffee is good I'm thinking, this coffee is good...

Then there's something going on across the street - two cars run into each other one cruising down Graham Avenue other guy coming up Kennedy, loud bang as their bumpers kiss and hide ain't nothing grand or dangerous but two fuckers come out, one an old guy in his sixties, other young dude 20-something backwards baseball hat baggy pants down to knees he screaming and panting and old guy giving it right back crowd in coffee shop gets excited crowd outside gather and pray and I watch thinking, oh no, oh no no no, what fresh new hell queen Dorothy Hudsucker you giveth me on this blue Tuesday, I decide to walk out and see what the fuck is the fuck and old guy shoves young guy baseball hat flying off his head, young guy pushes back sending old man to the pavement, I go running right into the fray and push young dude off - c'mon man, he's an old dude what the fuck - fuck him he pushed me first - but old man, see, he's insulted and indignant and he gets up fast and coming from over my shoulder I see a fist shoot forward aiming for the young guy missing but enraging the youngster then they are both screaming insults and threats and I stand between them one hand on each but both strong and determined and I am waving in the wind not wanting to see this old man get killed by this young gangster and not wanting to see my own middle-age ass stomped to the dirt, whoa, back and forth we go engines from both cars steaming in the light rain and we are panicking man, and while I scream for the gods to explain this bullshit to me I notice the crowd gathered around and they are laughing and cheering and showing me all of humanity in all its glory old man manages to slip under my arms and gets his hands on other guy's throat as a punch is thrown and old man's head snaps back but throws his own punch and nails the guy in the face now I'm once again in the middle and I am holding both apart with all my might and shoving one guy, then shoving the other, then some kid maybe 10 or 11 years old comes into the mix SMILING LIKE IT'S A GAME and I tell him to get the fuck out of here and he runs into his mom's arms as she gives me the finger, and I tell ya, all around there are people that will try to hold you down all day and every day but just keep the song "Back Door Man" by The Doors running in your head on a loop and you will be alright, sure, listen —

Now there are more people in the scene and some are even seriously concerned so I slide on out of there as I see a cop car coming into view siren red and blue and my signal to split, I sit on a corner tired middle-aged trembling hating people more and more but soon everything comes into focus and my hands stop shaking and I am alive and happy and it is time to move on, downtown mall spreads out on Portage Avenue city's main artery skyscrapers thrusting out from the sidewalk and charging at the clouds and there's a record store in the mall I always hang out at rain has stopped and I am starving for a continuance of things just as they are feeling alright and ready, I'm inside this ain't no normal mall it being the gateway to the ghetto ain't no scrabby middle-class parents with screaming kids in tow, ain't no suburban chicks talking about leather purses and jeweled mini-skirts, ain't no sweet heaven freckled-faced junior looking for blue skies, this is gang territory and the home of the wretched and ill-fated scruffs with front teeth missing, dirty sweat pants, minds gone running, and the smell of booze everywhere, the look of drugs at every corner, and the young girls are talking 'bout sex and violence, and the young men are waiting in darkened doorways, this is why I still come here I say though it's just for a glimpse, just a glimpse all I want these days of middle-age and boozy days and nights, I reach music store aisles of CD's and DVD's and graphic novels and posters and a small area of vinyl which is where I am flipping through records old and new but mostly old, hmmmm, got some Led Zeppelin, The Beatles, The Pixies, The White Stripes, The Tragically Hip, The Rezillos, The Dead Kennedys, Velvet Underground, The Stones with Mick and Keith on cover looking young and mean cigarette hanging from lips you can practically smell the Jack Daniels, got

'Never Mind The Bullocks' and 'London Calling' and quite a bit of shit I don't know,

"Hey buddy"

I turn towards the voice,

"Found what you're looking for?" He says, young clerk red curly hair disheveled leather band on wrist and sardonic wry grin but he seems all there when he speaks to me, know what I mean?

"Just looking around...actually, do you have any Ten Years After on vinyl?" I said,

"Yeah, I think so...looking for any album in particular?"

"Don't remember the name of the album, but it's the one with 'Going Home' on it, you know?"

"Yeah, that's the song with that crazy riff at the beginning, right?"

"Yeah..."

"Wasn't that the one they played at Woodstock?"

"I'm impressed, not going to lie to ya...."

"Yeah, I know, us millennials don't know shit...it's the internet and video games, man, they're fucking up our heads..."

"I said nothing, man..."

"Well, you're not wrong...for the most part... doesn't look like we got any Ten Years After...want to special order it?"

"No, it's alright...thanks, kid, keep listening to that good old music..."

"You know it. man..."

"Think I'll buy this Violent Femmes album..."

"Groovy"


There's this bookstore on Market Street among the cobblestone streets and multi-colored 19th century buildings of the Exchange District I'm walking up winding stairway everything creaky and old I can hear The Jesus And Mary Chain coming from upstairs reach store dusty hardwood floors and books, comics, records, head-shop paraphernalia I start looking around been hanging out at this place for over 30 years and the multicolored pipes of all sizes and shapes sit behind glass and shine and glow and go by like planets round the sun, movie posters on the walls range from B-movie cult stuff to foreign art flicks and there goes the 50 Foot Woman right beside The Bicycle Thief and there's a poster of Clarence Gatemouth Brown on the far wall playing his guitar with his black hat down just over his eyes, and the records here are much more alternative and indie than at that other place I've always dug that do-it-yourself thing, music, writing, painting, love the classic shit too as long as it's real and it rocks, good art is good art, but with the exception of the 60's and 70's the mainstream has always sucked just a bit more, hasn't it? Few people in store leave and the music changes to some Joe Strummer, 'Coma Girl', guy behind counter walks towards me black jeans and t-shirt short blonde hair going grey he's gaunt and thin and pale and here he comes,

"Ziggy, you old hippie" He says shaking my hand "Where you been, brother?"

"Been around, man, been around..."

He gives me a half-hug hand on shoulder this guy owner of store from very beginning turned me on to Jaime and Gilbert Hernandez when I was still reading superhero comics and that simple act changed everything,

"So how's business, Gord?"

"It's closing time, that's what I say..."

"You always close in mid-afternoon?"

"Whenever I feel like it, baby, my store...got some Johnny Walker downstairs...and some pretty damn fine dope"

"Lead the way"

Down the back stairs we go Gord an old crack-head and inner-city wanderer but managing somehow to leave the hard stuff behind sticking to the grass and booze and nothing else but journey to the depths had left its mark guy always sick and frail bad teeth the sadness just under the surface looks like old punk-rocker with too many gigs under his belt, we sit in basement damp and dim dirty couch and armchair feeling cool and easy he puts on some Mississippi Fred McDowell, a record, hear that needle scratch the surface and the blues slowly curling its way around the room, he gives me a short glass half-full of Scotch, one for him, lights a joint and passes it to me,

"How's married life treating you, Ziggy?"

"It's alright, my friend, it's alright (blowing out smoke)...you with anybody?"

Taking the joint, "Are you kidding? No serious shit for me, never again..."

"I hear ya"

"There is this broad though...we hang out together a lot, smoke dope, watch movies, go out dancing...sometimes we fuck, but not often..." He says sort-of sadly,

"Sounds cool to me, man. Shit, this weed tastes great!"

"I know, I know...ordered it online, can you believe it?"

"You get it in the mail?"

"Yeah, it's fucking great. Comes shrink-wrapped in these cool little packages, you wake up, yawn, go to your mailbox and grab your bag of goodies"

"How could it be anything but a good day after that?"

"Exactly...but brother, how is the writing going?"

"Really damn good...people seem to dig it, books are selling, just not enough to quit that shit job that I have, that shit job I've always had in one form or another..."

"You still night watchman at that museum?"

"Yeah, and the opera house"

"You work at two different places?"

"No, no, they're connected by an underground concourse, the opera house owns the museum...but I don't like it, man..."

"I thought it was pretty easy, that you dug it..."

"Not anymore...I just can't get past the fact that I still have to do these ridiculous jobs to get by after all these fucking years, that I can't do it with my writing alone, know what I mean?"

"Hey, it's about the art, isn't it? Besides, it shows commitment man, how many writers or musicians do you know that stick to it this long? You got stamina, baby!"

"That calls for a shot, what you got?"

"Ahh, let me see, some Sambuca?"

"Rock and roll!"

We do the shot and feel the burning all the way down -

"So what sells in your store anyway?" I say,

"You know the fuck these days, Ziggy, rap, hip-hop, pop..." He lights a cigarette, "Superhero movies, anything with zombies...I hate all that shit, especially that rap...hey, I got this new pressing of Charlie Parker, want to hear it?"

"Sure...which album?"

"It's from the Jazz Masters series...check out this groovy shit..."

And we listen and we smile and we drink talk and laugh and the smoke hangs in the air in deep purple puffs of cloud filling the room and our lungs and shortening our lives ever so sweetly, we're telling each other some sad tales about just livin' man and all the final goodbyes and sour-note happenings and lovely walks in the dark and remember when we did this, and when we did that, and what a fucker Big Bill was, do you remember old friend, and all that time still left ahead of us pulling away in one big motion of classical fuzz-box and that punk rock bar is still on Albert Street and that strip-joint with the fat lady singing still shines till midnight, it's saying 'come to me baby, come to the gypsy alleyways with your happy shoes on", so the sun crawls up the mountain and looks down from the peaks into the city and right down to this little neighborhood and shines its light on us and we is getting drunk right here and now and the beauty of being alive does not escape us, we say goodbye at the front door night coming quickly and we feel sad and happy man, sad that things have to end, happy that we had this moment, I wait for the bus I see a drunk passed out in the bus-shack the smell of stale liquor all around...


The streets go by in a blur through the ghetto-light and into what-comes-next and soon my working class neighborhood pulls up the sun sinking low and mean and the fall season turns the lights down just a bit everything yellow and gold and orange I see kids playing on a corner their parents annoying as ever and a dog barks and a car burns rubber and I approach my door, walk inside - Izzy sits there she's writing and she's beautiful her big brown eyes light up thick chestnut hair flowing down her shoulders I see the glow of booze on her cheeks and the bottle of beer beside her laptop and she's slightly buzzed, she hugs me our lips meeting in the middle,

"I'm writing and having a few drinks, just a few" She says,

"Have more than a few, baby...I love you when you're drunk..."

Tony Nesca was born in Torino, Italy in 1965 and moved to Canada at the age of three. He was raised in Winnipeg but relocated back to Italy several times until finally settling in Winnipeg in 1980. He taught himself how to play guitar and formed an original rock band playing the local bars for several years. At the age of twenty-seven he traded his guitar for a Commodore 64 and started writing seriously. He has published six chapbooks of stories and poems (which he used to sell straight out of his knapsack at local dives and bookstores), six novels, four books of poetry, one short story collection, and has been an active contributor to the underground lit scene for fifteen years, being published in innumerable magazines both online and in print. He currently resides in Winnipeg.